Be Mine

A billionaire marriage romance for adults

A complete marriage romance by bestselling author Katie Dowe.

Julian Robinson can't help but live up to the stereotype;

A billionaire playboy who always has a different woman on his arm.

That is, until Kymonia comes around!

Kymonia Blake is a successful novelist with no time for nonsense.

Fiction

Dowe, Katie

Be mine

[06/18]

So when Julian falls for her in a big way, he has a lot of convincing to do to show her she's the one he'll change his ways for.

The one, maybe, he would even make a life long commitment to.

But even if he finally manages to show Kymonia this, will Julian's playboy ways stay in the past where they belong?

Find out in this exciting and passionate marriage romance by Katie Dowe of BWWM Club.

Suitable for over 18s only due to sex scenes so hot, you'll need your own playboy billionaire to tame.

Get Free Romance eBooks!

Hi there. As a special thank you for buying this book, for a limited time I want to send you some great ebooks completely **free of charge** directly to your email! You can get it by going to this page:

www.saucyromancebooks.com/physical

You can see a the cover of these books on the next page:

These ebooks are so exclusive you can't even buy them. When you download them I'll also send you updates when new books like this are available.

Again, that link is:

www.saucyromancebooks.com/physical

Contents

Chapter 1

She was stuck! Kymonia sat back against the soft leather upholstery of her office chair and closed her eyes in frustration as if doing so would somehow bring to mind that she needed to write for the next very important scene. Her deadline was running out and she was stuck at the love scene of her current book and very soon she would have the editor breathing down her neck, albeit through the phone.

She was just not feeling the main characters. At first they had connected and things had been developing well until it was time for them to consummate the relationship and that's when she had become stuck in a hole. What had happened to the attraction that had sizzled between them every time they were within hairsbreadth of each other? She wondered, staring at the blinking cursor on her computer screen.

She had actually started with the chapter telling that the female character had started crying because she had discovered that her best friend had lied to her about something important and the male character had taken her into his arms to comfort her but that was where she was supposed to continue from but writer's block had settled in.

Kymonia had always wanted to be a writer. She had been a nerd at school who wore glasses and with her head constantly stuck inside a book. Even when she was supposed to be asleep she would be reading and when she was not reading she was dreaming. Her teachers had always told her that she was constantly up in the clouds and she was going to find herself spread-eagled on the ground because she never paid attention to where she was going.

Her two best friends: Marla and Gabrielle had been the popular and beautiful cheerleaders who had for some reason took her under their wings but had never quite managed to change how she looked and thought. They were very different yet they had maintained a friendship throughout the years that had taken them to college where Marla had studied fashion design and Gabrielle had become a lawyer. Kymonia had studied English Literature and Creative writing.

She had taught for two years after college but had quit to follow her dreams. She had changed into a tall elegant beauty that had stunned everyone around her including her friends. Two years ago she had had written her first bestseller: 'Woman in need' that had flown off the shelves in all the major bookstores in several countries and had catapulted her up to the best sellers list. She had followed up a year later with a poignant love story of a woman dying of a terminal cancer and the man who fell in love with her and stayed with her till the end. It had earned her quite a few awards and had been turned into a made for television movie soon after.

Now at age twenty-four, her reading community and her editor and publisher were pressuring her for something else to top those two books she had written and it was not happening. She had been at it for six months and it was slow going.

Her mother had called her earlier and invited her over for Sunday dinner with her and her stepfather but she had told her she was in the middle of writing. At the rate she was going maybe she should just give it a rest and go out and take a break, coming back with a fresh perspective.

Her father had died when she was just five years old and her mother had remarried five years after to a genial hardworking man who had never hesitated in giving her the love and care that she needed even though she was not his biological daughter. She called him pops, he was as pleased as punch that she did and they had gotten close over the years. She had bought them a house from her first royalty earnings and they were now living in a nice community where everyone knew each other and looked out for one another.

The phone rang just then and broke through her reverie. She uttered an impatient sigh as she realized that it was her editor Sylvia Bailey.

"Sylvia don't you take a day off?" Kymonia asked her mildly, getting ready to hear the same story. 'You need to meet your deadline.'

"Of course not darling," the woman responded and Kymonia could picture her amiable face and the constant cigarette at the side of her lips. "How else am I going to make sure my authors are doing their jobs and getting their creative juices flowing?"

Kymonia stifled the impatient retort that came to her lips. It was Sylvia who had looked at her unfinished manuscript and encouraged her to continue writing. She suggested the necessary changes to be made and because of that she had remained grateful to her. "I am working Syl, I have just reached a road block right now but I will get there."

"I have told you that you need to get your battery recharged darling," the woman told her impatiently. "When was the last time you had sex?"

"Excuse me?" Kymonia felt the startled laugh bubbling up inside her.

"Sex sweetie, the thing between a man and a woman that makes the world spin on its axis and sometimes manage to make you reach an orgasm." She sighed. "When was your last relationship?"

"I don't see why that has to do with anything," Kymonia told her firmly.

"Of course it has to do with everything! If you have not made love in a while how are you going to write a love scene?"

"By using the very vivid imagination God gave me," Kymonia told her, her hand rubbing her temple. She needed to end the conversation as soon as possible.

"That's not enough." The woman told her decisively. "I have just the thing; tickets to the opening of the trendy new restaurant uptown this Saturday. I will messenger them over to you tomorrow first thing. You could take your girlfriends with you and maybe you could find a man there who could give you enough sex to blow your mind and put you back on track."

"Let me get this straight: you want me to go out and find a random stranger to have sex with just to write my love scene?" Kymonia asked her incredulously.

"Of course not darling! Not any old stranger, maybe someone well known and not a pervert or a serial killer or both and wear something sexy, it helps." She hung up the phone before Kymonia could respond.

Kymonia sat there staring at the phone she had just put back into the cradle then she burst out laughing! The very idea that she should have sex just to be able to write her love scene was ludicrous to say the least! She had enough imagination for ten people and she was going to use it without having to use that means. She had often been asked about her love life when she had been interviewed and had always managed to sidestep the questions. How would it look for a writer of romantic fiction to have only had one disastrous relationship two years ago that had ended as soon as it had begun?

It had been her first year teaching at the local high school and he had been a fellow teacher who taught Science. She blinked as she remembered thinking that he was way too handsome to be teaching a subject like Science and he had laughed when she told him that. The relationship had blossomed quickly and she had envisioned herself getting married and settling down with him and raising kids together. She had given him her innocence without hesitation and he had taken her in his apartment while telling her that she was the only one for him. It had taken a month for her to realize that he had been sleeping with most of the female teachers on staff. That had been part of the reason why she had left without looking back and she had never entered into another relationship since.

Gabrielle and Marla had told her not to let that creep be the reason why she never had a relationship, that would be giving him too much power but she could not help herself, now she was being very cautious.

She stood up and stretched languidly padding over to the balcony to look at her tomato plants to see how they were progressing. It was almost the end of summer and it had rained earlier in the day. The droplets were still on the leaves making them glisten in the fading sunlight. She had bought an actual house a year ago with yard space and very near to a wooded area that led to an old abandoned building that was slated to be demolished the next two weeks. Sometimes when she needed outdoor space she would take her laptop and a picnic basket and would sit and write until the sun went down. Until she could not see properly and only then she would head back to the house to see the light on her machine blinking like crazy.

Marla and Gabrielle had often told her that the abandoned building was probably home to creeps and weirdoes and she should have better sense than to leave her perfectly safe home to go into a building that was also probably a rapists' pad. She had laughed and told them that she was perfectly capable of taking care of herself.

The house was a charming split level building with mellow brick walls and glass doors and windows to capture the light of the sun. It had three bedrooms, two baths, a work office that she had designed herself, and a kitchen/dining area and a living room. She had made some alterations and added a fireplace in the living room that she lit whenever it got cold. She hardly used the modern kitchen, sometimes forgetting to eat when she was writing and usually had several take out leaflets on her fridge to order out. Her friends were always coming around to check up on her and bemoan the fact that she had chosen to live in the countryside.

She waved to her next door neighbor Mrs. Willows who lived alone since her husband had died ten years ago. The woman was sometimes too friendly and intrusive but she had gotten used to her and did not let her bother her too much, she supposed the woman was a bit lonely and needed company.

"My dear, I had no idea you were at home," she said wandering over to the tall wire fence that separated their yards. "I came out here several times hoping to see you and I did not see evidence of you being here."

"I was trying to do some work Mrs. Willows," she told the woman with a smile. Her friends said she was a nosy busy body and stayed away from her whenever they came around but Kymonia liked her. She was almost eighty but looked strong and was still erect with her wispy white blond hair and watery blue eyes and shriveled white skin.

"How is it going?" she had been so fascinated when the girl had moved in and she had discovered that she was the bestselling author she had read about in the papers.

"It's going," Kymonia said with a shrug. "How are you?"

"I am as well as can be considering," she answered. "I made a whole dish of lasagna enough to feed the entire neighborhood and I was wondering if you wanted some?" There was a hopeful look on the woman's elderly face.

"Of course, you know I cannot say no to your delicious cooking. I will be right over."*****

"Do you know whose restaurant this is?" Gabrielle exclaimed looking at the embossed invitations for the opening. They were at their usual restaurant having lunch together where they tried to meet once every week. Gabrielle had just left court and looked cool and attractive in an expensive dark blue skirt suit with a white silk inside blouse. Her chic bob brushed against her cocoa brown face and her make-up was flawless.

"Whose?" Kymonia asked indifferently, digging into her fries which she had smothered ketchup all over.

"Girlfriend you are killing me," Marla sighed theatrically shaking her flamboyant blonde wig. She was wearing something she had designed and it was in bright colors and fitted her tall voluptuous body like a glove. "This is one of Julian Robinson's projects. You do know who Julian Robinson is don't you?"

"Isn't he the guy who went to space?" Kymonia said with a straight face as her friends looked at her as if she was from space. "I am kidding! I have heard of Julian Robinson, billionaire extraordinaire who makes money with everything he touches."

"Oh thank goodness!" Gabrielle exclaimed. "There is hope for you yet."

"Thank you," Kymonia said dryly. "So you guys up for it?"

"You don't need to ask me twice," Gabrielle said with a sigh, digging into her salad with a lack of enthusiasm. She had put herself on a strict diet because boyfriend of the month had told her that she had put on a little weight. "I need to unwind and forget about men and work and the fact that the prosecutor is kicking my black ass in court."

"That bad huh?" Marla said sympathetically. "I myself need to get laid. Ever since I broke up with Tyler a month ago I have not had any action and I am beginning to feel withdrawals in that direction and the fashion line I am doing now is going quite well. How is the book coming along?" she turned to Kymonia.

"Not very well," she answered with a shrug. After a very filling dinner with Mrs. Willows yesterday she had gone back over to the house and tried again but had come up with zero, so instead she had taken out a book from her well stocked bookcase and curled up on the couch and read until almost midnight. She told her friends what Sylvia had said to her.

After the general laughter Gabrielle said, "I think she is right. You have not had a relationship since that creep at the school you used to teach and you need to experience it in order to write it, don't you?"

"You are siding with Sylvia by agreeing that I need to have sex?" Kymonia looked at her friend incredulously.

"I just think you need to find someone, girlfriend," Gabrielle told her. "You are too buried in your work and believe me when I say it; work is not all you need to get out there."

"I agree, we are not getting any younger." Marla said with a grin revealing white teeth spaced at the front.

"Speak for yourself," Kymonia threw a fry in her direction. "I have a vivid imagination and I will make it work.

*****

"I know Mom and I am sorry but I promise to come over as soon as I can." Kymonia promised mopping her face that was dripping with sweat after her thirty minute run in the neighborhood.

She had been doing a lot of different techniques to get her creative juices flowing but so far it has been four days and she was still stuck right where she had been Sunday.

"Honey your dad and I have not seen you in three weeks and we miss you." Gloria exclaimed.

"I know mom, I miss you too." Kymonia sank down on the shiny hardwood floor and started doing her stretches.

"How is the book coming?" she asked.

Kymonia flopped back against the pillows she had piled on the floor and closed her eyes. She wished people would stop asking her that.

"It's going Mom, that's one of the reasons why I have not been around; you know how it is when I get caught up."

"I know dear and I do hope you are not still going up to that old abandoned place, I worry about you." Her mother said in concern.

"Mom, don't worry about me." She said reassuringly. "I promise I will drop by as soon as I can. Where is Pops?" she asked fondly.

"In the garden tinkering." There was a smile in her mother's voice. "He just reaped some carrots and tomatoes yesterday and has gone out to look at the cucumbers he had planted."

"I knew he had a green thumb," Kymonia said with a laugh. "Tell him that thanks to him my tomatoes are looking healthy. Are you guys okay? I mean do you need anything?"

"Honey we are fine!" Her mother told her. "You have done so much already and we are so grateful."

"My pleasure Mom," Kymonia told her sincerely.

"All right dear, I love you and make sure you eat."

"I will and I love you too, kiss Pops for me."

She stretched out her legs wearily to get rid of the sudden cramp in her thigh and lay there for a minute thinking.

She was still trying to get used to her trim svelte body after being called chubby all through high school and then hitting college where the running up and down from one class to another and eating on the run had slimmed her down considerably. She had exchanged her old fashioned glasses for contact lenses that actually highlighted her dark brown eyes. She had suddenly gained chiseled cheekbones or killer cheekbones as her friends had called them and teamed with her full lips and her oval shaped face she had turned into a raving beauty almost overnight that had been called: 'The Beauty with the power of the pen' by the press.

She let her mind drift for a while and then she got up and headed for the bathroom. She had to get some work done today.

*****

Julian Robinson dragged his fingers through his already tousled dark hair and sat on the side of the bed. He was getting tired of waking up beside a strange woman each time. He had met her at a cocktail function and he had taken her home with him because he had been attracted to her at the moment. But after the sex, he had found that he was not interested any more. He had told her politely that he would be in touch but they both knew that was not true.

It was two a.m. on a Monday morning and he needed to get some sleep because he wanted to be in the office first thing. Both his mother and father expected him to find someone suitable and settle down but so far he had not adhered to their wish. His father was the CEO of Robinson's Holdings and he was second in command. The press referred to him as the billionaire playboy whose looks and wealth gave him easy access to life. He knew he had to change that image if he wanted to be taken seriously in the business world, he knew it without his father constantly drumming it into his head.

He had been born with the veritable silver spoon in his mouth and had been spoiled by both parents who had discovered that he was going to be it in terms of them reproducing and they had showered everything on him. He had gone through life with a careless persona which had not been helped because he also happened to have a brilliant mind. He had never known hardship in his life and women fought over themselves to be with him. He had also never been in a serious relationship. His 'love affairs' usually lasted two weeks at the most but when he had touched his twenty-seven years in June he had realized that he needed more and he was getting tired of women who made it so easy for him to be with them, he wanted a challenge.

He switched on the light and booted up his laptop. He had seen a half demolished hotel in a prime location downtown just last week and had spoken to his father about acquiring it. He just needed to do the background check and find out more about the ownership side of it before he put it to the board. He could already see in his mind's eye the sort of majestic building it would be already and he was determined to get it. Besides it would be an excellent source of employment for the people in that area. Maybe a family hotel? No the location was not right. More like a hotel to house business men and a section for their wives to shop and do the necessary things women seemed to be interested in. He quickly made a note to himself in order to be reminded of the idea he had just had.

Chapter 2

Kymonia applied her make-up carefully, paying special attention to the eye shadow she was putting on her lids. She had chosen to wear a clinging green dress with a modest neckline and a deep cut down the center of her back that restricted her from wearing a bra and even panties. It had been an impulse buy and she had never worn it yet but felt the material touched her body like a loving hand. She wore gold accessories and slid her feet into black high heels. She had piled her unruly curls in a careless bun on top of her head and allowed a few tendrils to drift along her cheeks and at the back of her neck.

She was meeting her friends at the restaurant and a quick glance at the clock showed her that it was almost nine p.m.

She grabbed her car keys from the hook and headed for the door.

*****

"This place is a crush," Gabrielle complained as they made their way over to where they could find a suitable spot to be so that they could see what was happening around them. She was wearing an ice blue gown that looked very good on her.

"And look at all the brothers around," Marla said practically smacking her lips. She was dressed in one of her designs; an outrageous pink and orange dress that hugged her voluptuous figure and revealed a lot more than it covered.

Waiters were weaving their way through the crowd, serving entrees and champagne and other wines and there was a lot of laughter and muted conversation going on. A waiter came around to their section and they chose tiny tomato tarts and mushroom puffs. The place was elegant and the lighting muted, it had been a rundown fast food restaurant and looking at it now, one could not tell that it had had the paint peeling on the interior walls and the floor with its chipped ceramic tiles. Now the walls had been covered with a bold red and black paint slashed across the surface as if an angry child had wanted to do some damage or had been acting out but it gave the place an ultra modern look that had actually worked.

"I am getting a little thirsty and I see that they have an open bar so I am going to indulge a little," Kymonia told her friends.

"In the meantime we are going to show ourselves to some brothers to see what might happen." Marla said with a grin dragging Gabrielle off with her.

Kymonia made her way towards the long curved bar and sat on one of the stools gratefully, signaling the bartender to get her tonic water.

She was sipping the liquid and looking around curiously, taking in the well dressed women and the smartly dressed men when she felt a presence beside her. She did not turn around, deliberately ignoring whoever it was that had taken the stool beside her.

"A dry martini for me and another gin and tonic for the beautiful lady Jerome," a deep voice murmured beside her.

"Yes sir."

She turned just then and recognized him from the pictures constantly in the papers. "Nothing for me Jerome, I have barely started this drink as it is." She told the bartender, her tone cool.

"If I cannot buy you a drink then how about a dance or a drive along the shores?" he asked her, his emerald green eyes meeting hers.

"Not interested one way or another Mr. Robinson." She told him coolly.

"You know who I am but I don't know your name. I seem to recognize the face from somewhere but I can't remember where I met you before." Julian said with a charming smile. He was handsome! No wonder women threw themselves at him, she thought objectively

"Don't you have to go around the room and mingle?" she asked him mildly, not in the least bit impressed by his looks and the fact that he was touted as being one of the richest young men in the world. He was far from being her type.

"I have already done my duty now it's time for pleasure and being with you is quite a pleasure," he grinned to reveal perfectly white teeth and a dimple in one cheek.

"Do women actually fall for that tired line?"

"Ouch!" he held a hand against his heart as if she had mortally wounded him. "Apparently not. How about telling me your name and we get out of here?"

"Mr. Robinson I don't do one night stands and I am just here by the bar because I wanted a little quiet time and you are spoiling that for me." She told him pointedly.

Jerome had returned with his drink and went off to serve somebody else by this time. "I am not going to apologize and I would still like to know your name."

Before she could respond a pretty and well dressed blonde rushed over to her. "Kymonia Blake!" she gushed. "I have read your books so many times that I know them almost word for word and the movie was brilliant! Julian you did not tell me you know Kymonia," she ended with a pout of her cherry red lips.

"I am just realizing who she is," his tone was amused as recognition dawned in his eyes. "My mother is a fan."

"My name is Katy," the blonde stuck out her hand for it to be shaken and Kymonia took it in hers.

"Nice to meet you." She told the woman politely.

"May I have your autograph?"

"Of course," she said with a smile.

She hurriedly search inside her little clutch and came out with a small notepad. "The first page will do."

Kymonia scribbled something on the page and signed her name at the bottom. The woman did not stop there. She handed her phone to Julian for him to take a picture of her hugging Kymonia which he did with a smile and handed the phone back to Katy.

"Thank you so much," she gushed before going off.

"A romance novelist," he murmured sipping his martini and looking at her above the glass. "Does that mean you are versed in the art of lovemaking?"

"My imagination serves me well Mr. Robinson," she answered coolly, wondering why out of all the women he had zeroed in on her.

"It's actually Julian." He told her. "I am curious. Who do you base your characters on?"

"Are you really interested in my work or are you just trying to make conversation?" she countered. "As far as I can tell you have never actually read any of my books have you?"

"I intend to as soon as I get home. Pity my mother is out of town she would have loved to meet you. So how about going out with me tomorrow night?" he placed his empty glass on the countertop and looked at her, his green gaze holding hers.

"No," she answered promptly. "Goodnight Mr. Robinson, lovely restaurant." She hurried over to where her friends were talking to a group of guys.

"Ready?" she asked them as soon as she greeted the men.

"Was that Julian Robinson you were talking to at the bar?" Marla asked her curiously.

"Yes." She answered briefly.

"What did he say to you?" Gabrielle stared at her curiously.

"He said his mother is a fan," she put the stole around her and headed for the exit with her friends trailing behind her.

"That was a pretty long conversation you guys were having," Marla persisted catching up to her.

"It was not," Kymonia protested. "He just wanted to know how I came to start writing romance, that's all."

*****

Julian watched her leave, his eyes following her progress as the two women walked behind her. She was beautiful, he thought and he wanted to get to know her better. He was not used to women turning him down and he had felt a grudging admiration for her when she had done so. She had an incredibly sexy walk and that dress with the deep plunge at the back showed her beautiful coffee and cream complexion to its best advantage.

He sat there on the stool with her exotic scent lingering behind and realized that the pleasure had gone out of the evening as far as he was concerned. He looked around and waved to several business acquaintances and his eyes sought the place where he had left his date for the night. She was nowhere to be seen and he wondered absently where she had wandered off to. She was a model who he called every now and then when he needed a companion to attend a function and she had never told him no, not even when she was seeing someone. Right now he just wanted to get the hell out of here and go home.

*****

"What's the latest?" Sylvia asked her without preamble.

"And good day to you too," Kymonia said cheerfully.

"I am in over my head with bad manuscripts and I have been editing a piece of crap that should really be thrown in the garbage but there is a glimmer of potential somewhere deep down under all the misspellings and grammatical errors so I am doing my best not to tear it into shreds and say the hell with it. I am taking a break from what is now becoming the worst week of my career to find out if my bestselling author is anywhere near to completing her perfectly delightful manuscript."

"Wow!" Kymonia said sympathetically. "Since you put it that way I am going to give you the good news that I have been writing up a storm and I am halfway there."

"Good," the woman said with a heavy sigh. "That is good news and now I can go back to the thrash I am editing with a clear head and maybe do a bit of good. Oh by the way, you did not tell me how you enjoyed the opening on Saturday?"

"It was okay, I guess."

"More than okay if you managed to catch the eyes of Julian Robinson." Sylvia said smugly. "I told you to go get yourself a man and see what happens and you managed to go and get the cream of the crop."

"What are you talking about?" Kymonia asked her puzzled.

"He called the publishing house asking about you." She clarified.

"And what did you tell him?"

"He wanted your book darling and more specifically he want a signed copy of it and he is willing to pay twice the amount it costs." Sylvia said in satisfaction. "So I am having it messengered to your house for you to sign and send it to him."

"Don't you have signed copies there?" she asked impatiently.

"He wants it personalized darling and we are talking about Julian Robinson whose company happens to own a piece of Pearl Publishing House so anything to please that man."

"Okay fine."

"You made quite an impression it seems." Sylvia told her.

"I am sure I did," Kymonia said dryly.

"Okay girl I am not going to keep you any longer. Talk to you."

*****

He pursued her. She had received the copy of her book and had hesitated awhile not knowing what to write in it until she had just written: 'To Julian Robinson with my regard'; and had sent it off. She knew it was probably not what he wanted to see written there but that had been the point.

He called her as soon as he received it and she did not even bother to ask how he had gotten her number.

"That was a pretty impersonal note," he said in a slow drawl.

"I don't know you at all Mr. Robinson," she answered not pretending that she did not know who it was.

"And I want to change that," he murmured. "Have dinner with me later,"

"The answer is no," she told him firmly. "It might come as a shock to you but not all women find you irresistible."

"It is a shock to me Kymonia," he told her in amusement. "Tell me what I can do to become more attractive to you."

"Nothing. I am not interested and I really need to get back to work now." She told him.

"I need to write you a check for the book and I want to deliver it myself." He persisted.

"Write the check to the publishing house."

"I have been thinking about you a lot since I saw you that night and I really need to see you." He said seriously.

"Mr. Robinson you have your pick of women and I am sure if you search through you will find more than a few who are quite ready to fall at your feet."

"I can but I want to go out with you." He told her softly.

"I don't go out with men who treat women like possessions to discard as they see fit. You have quite a reputation and I would be a fool to want to join the harem you have going on." She said coolly. "I am not desperate."

"You don't think very much of me do you?" he asked her wryly. "No, I don't but my opinion should not matter. There are plenty of others who I am sure think the world of you."

"What if I am a changed person?" he asked her half jokingly.

"A leopard cannot change its spots Mr. Robinson, now I really have to go." She hung up on him.

*****

Julian sat back against the chair in contemplation. He had been talking to himself and wondering if it was the fact that she had rejected him as to why he was so interested but he had an idea it was not that. He had not been able to stop thinking about her and picturing how she had looked at the bar and when she was leaving.

He had started reading the book and had found out that she was a very good writer who paid attention to detail and had you gripped from the very first page. His buzzer sounded just then and he realized that it was his father's private number. "Yes Dad?"

"The former owners of the pharmaceutical company are planning to sue us for what they claimed to be coercion by our acquisition team so we need to be prepared." James Robinson told him briefly.

"This does not need to go to court Dad, we have the papers here that they signed off on the deal and they willingly collected the money we paid them which was more than generous considering." Julian said a little impatiently.

"I know that son but the old man is saying that he was quite intimidated by you and you ran roughshod over him so he was in fear of his life."

"Are you kidding me?" Julian's voice was incredulous. "I spoke to the man in front of his two sons and told him that we had no intention of doing away with the company we just wanted to make it better and more viable and he sat right there and agreed."

www.SaucyRomanceBooks.com/RomanceBooks

"I know," James' voice was soothing. "To be on the safe side, I want you to get ready and arm yourself with every documentation and have our lawyers look them over to make sure we did not miss anything."

"Will do Dad," Julian said with a shake of his head.

"And son," his father continued. "Your mother and I are expecting you home for dinner tonight. She has not seen you properly since we came back from Europe on Sunday."

"I have been working late Dad, you know that, but of course I will be there for dinner." Julian paused a little bit. "Dad how did you know that mom was the right one for you when you met her?"

There was silence on the other end and he could just see the expression on his father's face.

"You have met someone significant?"

"I think so but she won't give me the time of day." He said ruefully.

"Ah finally a woman who puts up some resistance, that's great and it will do you a world of good. I knew your mother was the

Page 39

one because I fell in love with her the first time I saw her in the hallway in college. The only thing was I was too timid to approach her until I almost lost her to someone else."

"So you worked up the courage to ask her out?" Julian said in amusement.

"My palms were sweating," he said with a laugh. "Who is this young lady who has caught your attention?"

"Her name is Kymonia Blake and she is a novelist."

"Your mother is a fan of hers, quite a beautiful and talented young woman." His father mused. "Have you asked her out?"

"She wants nothing to do with me I am afraid."

"You will find a way son, you always do."

*****

He sent her flowers, lots of them which included petunias, gardenias and roses in different colors. The card read: "I am going to change and be worthy of your attention." She started to tear up the card but changed her mind and placed it inside her desk drawer and put the flowers into a huge vase and placed it on her desk, no use wasting perfectly good floral arrangements.

He called her again but this time he had changed his tactics. He spoke to her about the book he was reading and asked her about the main characters and she found herself talking to him about it. At the end of the conversation she realized that he had not mentioned going out with him.

His next gift was a beautifully embossed personal diary with the note: 'For you to write down your personal feelings when you don't feel like writing.'

*****

"He keeps sending me gifts and has been hounding me to go out with him at first but now he just calls and talk about my book and ask about my day and how my writing is progressing like he wants to be my friend." Kymonia put the tray of hot chocolate on the table in front of the circular settee and sat beside her friends.

It was a Saturday and they had come over for refreshment and conversation and to drag their friend away from her writing for a little bit. She still had not made it over to her mom's house and she was starting to feel bad about it. It had been two weeks since she had met Julian and he had been in constant touch with her.

"So go out with him," Gabrielle said sensibly. She had kicked off her sneakers and made herself comfortable by curling her feet under her. Marla as usual was in flaming red hot pants and a billowing purple blouse and this time she was wearing a red wig.

"I will not!" Kymonia retorted. "He has more women than I have shoes and you know how many shoes I have."
"Maybe he has changed his wicked ways," Marla said with a grin.

"I strongly doubt that," Kymonia said dryly nibbling on the cookies Mrs. Willows had made for her. "I find that strangely enough I am getting to like his conversation. Apart from his being a womanizer, he is quite a good conversationalist."

"That's where it starts," Gabrielle warned her.

"Where what starts?"

"Good conversation often leads to incredible sex and before you know it you end up doing it every day." She said with confidence.

"The guy you met at the restaurant opening?" Kymonia asked shrewdly.

"Yes," Gabrielle threw up her hands in disgust. "We started talking about the environment, he is an environmentalist lawyer and then courtroom maneuvers and before you know it we were naked in bed together and going at it like rabbits."

"Sounds like you had a good time so what's the problem?" Marla asked her.

"I don't know if I want to see him again and he keeps calling me." She admitted.

"What's wrong with him?" Kymonia asked her curiously.

"He still lives with his mother."

"Ouch," Marla said with a delicate shudder. "Run far away from him honey, he clearly has difficulties cutting the umbilical cord."

"I tried telling myself that but then I weaken when he calls. I am resolute that I would tell him I don't want to see him until he comes over and we start going at it again. He is huge and he knows how to handle himself." She said with a sigh.

"Do you know we are sounding more and more like brothers every day?" Kymonia asked them looking at both girls.

"Oh Lord you are right!" Gabrielle exclaimed. "Time to tune in to some Lifetime movies, which will put us back on track."

Chapter 3

Her fingers flew over the keyboard as the inspiration flew through her mind. She had woken up at five a.m. this morning with the chapter drumming inside her head. She had to forgo her usual run, had grabbed a cup of steaming black coffee and started writing. She was still at it and it was a little past ten. She finally ran out of steam at some minutes past eleven and she took up her coffee cup to find that the coffee had gotten ice cold. She had not bothered to take a shower but had dragged on old sweat bottoms and an even older T-Shirt and her hair was piled on top of her head haphazardly. She had vaguely heard her phone ringing but had not answered any of them and now she realized that she had received calls from her mother, Gabrielle and Marla and Julian had been the last call.

She was just about to take a shower and get herself something to eat when the front doorbell pealed causing her to jump. She hurried to see who it was and to her surprise she realized it was Julian. What was he doing here? He had stopped asking her out even though he called her everyday. She had started to think his interests had waned. She was certainly not dressed for company and by the looks of him he looked as handsome as usual in a dark green sweater over a white shirt with a red tie and his dark hair was tousled by the breeze.

"Julian what are you doing here?" she asked through the door.

"I come bearing breakfast. It tried calling you and I know you have probably been writing and forgot to eat." His deep voice called out to her.

"What's for breakfast?" she asked him.

"Impossibly delicate croissants, scrambled eggs and bacon and piping hot coffee from the best café in town and some fruits as well." He told her.

"Okay I am convinced." She slid back the lock and let him in. He took in her attire and realized that even though she was not wearing a stitch of make-up and her clothes were old and shabby she still managed to look beautiful.

"Where do you want me to set it up?" he asked coming inside and taking a quick sweeping view of the elegant place.

"Follow me," she led him into the kitchen and he put the package on the counter. "I take it you have invited yourself for breakfast as well?" she asked reaching into the cupboard for some plates.

"I ate something very early and I am feeling a little hungry," he gave her a winning smile.

"How did you know I have not eaten?" she asked him sitting on the stool opposite to him.

"You told me in one of our conversations that when the creative juice was flowing you forget to eat." He accepted a plate from her and started eating.

"Thanks I really appreciate this." She bit into the delicate flaky croissant and her eyes widened. "This is delicious!"

"I told you," he said with a boyish grin. "Our chef at home makes the best ones."

"You brought these from home?" she looked at him curiously. "So you left the office and went back home to get these?"

"Not quite I am afraid," he told her. "I had one of the drivers go for them and carried them to the office."

"I see," she said quietly and even though she did not elaborate he knew what she was thinking.

"I don't take advantage of the employees Kym," he told her seriously. "He happened to be going to the house to pick up some files there as well." He told her feeling that he had to explain things to her.

"It's not my place to criticize, I am sorry," she had polished off the delicious pastry and was eating her eggs and bacon. "I wish I knew how to make eggs this good." She added.

"Clyde, our chef makes the best of everything; maybe you could ask him to teach you someday." He told her.

"What are you doing Julian?" she asked him suddenly. "You are wealthy and totally hot and I am sure you are not used to this, so why are you doing it?"

"Because I want to show you that I am changing," he said with a little quirk of his lips.

"Why?"

"Isn't it obvious?" he had stopped eating and his eyes met hers, their meaning clear. "You want a man who does not treat women like possessions and treats her with respect and I am showing you that I can be that man."

"I am not interested in a relationship Julian," she told him honestly. "I don't want you to change because of me."

"I want to be your friend," he reached out to take the hand on the counter and Kymonia felt a jolt go through her at his touch. "Let's be friends for now."

"And you are satisfied with that?" she asked him looking at him doubtfully.

"For now," he turned her hand around and opened it to look at her palm. "I have not been with anyone since I have met you and I am willing to let you set the pace."

Kymonia felt her heart shift inside her breasts at his words and she could not speak for a little bit. "You can't put that on me Julian," she whispered wanting to take her hand away from his.

"I am not putting anything on you, I just want to be around you as a friend until you tell me otherwise, can you give me that?"

he asked her huskily, taking her hand to his lips and kissing the palm, sending a tingle through her.

She nodded and he put her hand down. "Good now I have to go, I have a meeting in twenty minutes."

"Oh!" she could not believe how disappointed she felt.

"Don't worry just say the word and I will bring dinner over later." He said hopefully watching her face.

"No," she shook her head. "I have to go and see my parents later for a long overdue visit."

"Okay maybe tomorrow then." He kissed her softly on the cheek before striding towards the door. He tilted her chin to look at her. "Go back and write," he told her softly before leaving.

Kymonia stood there staring after him and he turned back and gave her a wave before driving off. She closed the door and wandered over to her desk but for a long time she just sat there and did not write anything.

*****

"This is very good Mom," Kymonia said sincerely as she bit into the tasty meatloaf. She had not exactly lied to Julian about her coming over to visit her mother and stepfather but she had not done so when she told him she would. She had gotten caught up in her writing and by the time she looked at the clock it was some minutes to nine and she had just gotten something to eat and then gone to bed. So she had put away writing from early in the afternoon and made a conscious decision to make time and here she was.

"Thanks dear," Gloria Rollins said with a smile as she reached for the vegetable platter. Her husband Daniel was sitting at the head of the table with one eye glued to the large screen television in the living room.

"Pops I see you are otherwise occupied," Kymonia said with a teasing smile.

"I just want to see who is winning," he said with a sheepish smile, glancing at his wife. "We miss you coming around honey; don't take so long to visit."

"I know and I promise to do better. You know me when I get caught up with my writing how time slips away from me."

"So you are back on track?" her mother asked her.

"I am," she said with a nod. "I have a few chapters left and I am playing around with the ending."

"My daughter the famous author," her mother said with a shake of her head. "Who would have thought it."

*****

"How was the visit with your parents?" Julian called her as soon as she got home and was having a cup of tea. The wind had picked up in the evening and for mid September it had gotten quite cold.

"It was okay, thanks." She had been looking forward to him calling and maybe if he had not she would have called. "How are you?"

"I am still at the office trying to sort out some things for court." He had told her about the lawsuit that the company was up against.

"I thought you did not have to go to court," Kymonia settled down behind her desk with the intention of doing some writing before going to bed.

"We thought so as well but no amount of talking to the persons involved has budged them so far," he told her with a sigh and she could just imagine him running his fingers through his dark hair. She had started revising her opinion about him and looked forward each day to their conversations.

"I am sorry Julian but I am sure your very efficient lawyers know what they are doing." She told him soothingly.

"So how are you really?" he asked her softly. It was a strange experience for him being friends with her and even stranger for him being without a woman for a whole month.

"I am okay and I am getting somewhere with my book now. Do you still want to go out to dinner?" she asked him suddenly.

"Of course," he forced himself to remain calm. He had decided that he was not going to ask her again for awhile. "What do you have in mind?"

"Somewhere quiet," she suggested. "I don't want people seeing us and making a big deal out of it."

"I know just the place," he told her quickly. "And you don't have to dress up much. What time should I pick you up?"

"Julian it's not like it's a date," she warned him. "I just need to get out of the house for a little bit. I think I am beginning to catch the color of the paint. We are friends right?"

"Yes, we are," he agreed, quietly warning himself that he had to be patient. He was up for the challenge so this should not be very hard. "I will pick you up at eight."

*****

"What's going on with you?" Sheeree McAllister was a well renowned model who had traveled all over the world on different shoots and had been on again off again girlfriend of Julian's for the past year and a half. They had an understanding that when she was in town they would be exclusive but now she had arrived this morning from Trinidad where she had been for the last three weeks doing a swimsuit shoot only to have Julian tell her that it was over. She had come straight from the airport to his office and had been sent in by his secretary. She was a coolly beautiful brunette with hazel eyes and sharp cheekbones that had earned her many covers on the most prestigious magazines. He had often wondered why he had never fallen in love with her.

www.SaucyRomanceBooks.com/RomanceBooks

"I need something more Sheeree," he had stood up and come from around the desk to greet her, kissing her cheeks lightly and breathing in her subtle expensive scent. She was wrapped from head to toe in black that looked startling against her very white skin.

She moved away from him and went and sat on one of the sofas in the room. "Someone I know?" she asked mildly amused, knowing that he was going to be running back to her eventually, he always did.

"That does not matter right now," he told her stiffly, hating her condescending manner. "The point is I want this to work and I am willing to give up whatever it takes to make it work."

"Darling are you listening to yourself?" she crossed her long legs in confidence. "You have never been able to stay with one woman for more than a week, I am the only constant relationship you have and even so, ours is not what people would call normal. What are you trying to prove?"

"I care about this girl Sheeree and I would like a chance to see it work," he said a little grimly knowing what she said was what she knew him to be. Most of it was true but he aimed to prove her and others wrong about him not being able to change.

"Okay darling, you know I am available when you come to your senses. I will be in town for a week so call me." She stood up gracefully and came towards him. "I like what we have and it works so I want to hang on to it." She kissed him lightly on the mouth and usually that would have been the catalyst that would have him pulling her into his arms but this time he just stepped back not feeling anything.

"I am not going to call Sheeree, this is serious and I am going to allow anyone to mess with it."

*****

"What do you know of me?" They were at the restaurant and were eating the meal of curried lobster and white rice that had been brought to them. The place was small and intimate and there were very few people sitting down to have a meal.

"I know you are quite the businessman," Kymonia said lightly trying to gauge his mood. He had picked her up and apart from asking how she was he had been very quiet. "I was reading in the papers how you made that hotel downtown into quite a showpiece and the restaurant that opened a month ago is quite successful."

"You sound like the P.R. firm we have on staff," he told her dryly.

"What's going on Julian?" she asked him. He looked at her for a moment, noticing not for the first time how the red silk shirt she had on looked good against her skin and her black hair had been caught up in a ponytail that made her look like a teenager.

"I have never been friends with someone I am interested in before." He told her bluntly, his green gaze meeting her dark brown ones. "I never invested in a relationship because I never had to and I find it strange. I am attracted to you and it is more than that." He paused and took one of her hands in his. "Someone I used to see told me that I will never change, what do you think?"

"I don't know you well enough to say whether or not you will," she told him honestly, feeling the frisson of desire going through her at his touch. She would have probably let him make love to her but he had not mentioned it to her and she was not modern enough to bring it up herself.

"I spent my adult years and even when I was a teenager, I had women throwing themselves at me so it became easy," he smiled grimly. "This is a first for me and I don't know how to behave around you sometime. I don't know if I try to kiss you if I would be stepping over the boundaries there are between us."

"Kissing is allowed," she told him softly. "I am not ready for a relationship yet Julian so I really appreciate your friendship. I am totally wrapped up in my writing and sometimes as you know, I forget to eat. That would not be fair to another person so that is one reason why I have stayed away from relationships until now."

"What are you saying to me Kym?" he asked her, their meals forgotten.

"I am saying that I am not saying yes and I am not saying no. I am simply saying that we should see where this is going if you can put up with the way I am."

"I am willing to put up with anything from you as long as I get to be with you," he told her softly. He pulled his hand away from her and Kymonia stared at him in surprise. "Our meals are getting cold."

They talked about everything and he told her about his trips abroad and the time he went to Jamaica for a week.

"I have never been there and I was planning to base one of books on a Caribbean island but have not decided which one yet." She told him sipping the white wine he had ordered with the meal.

"I spent time in Montego Bay and one day I hope I will be able to take you there."

"I would like that very much." She told him.

*****

"When are we going to meet her?" his mother came inside his bedroom after a discreet knock on the door. He had taken Kymonia home half an hour ago and given her a chaste kiss on the lips and drove away but not before making sure that she was safely inside the house. He knew she had been expecting him to do much more but he had restrained himself, barely and now he was suffering for it. He had come straight up to his suite and had changed out of his clothes and pulled on loose pajama bottoms and was in bed reading the book she had autographed, he was at the love scene and he was getting hard reading and thinking about her.

"Who?" Julian put aside the book and gave his mother his full attention. She was a very beautiful woman with dark brown hair tinted with red and green eyes that he had inherited from her and she defined the word elegant.

"Don't play dense with me Jules," she reprimanded him gently, sitting on the side of his king sized bed and folding her hands on her lap. He had never introduced any of the women he slept with to either his mother or his father preferring to be sure that that woman would be around for longer than a month. "You have been seeing one of my favorite authors for some time now and I have yet to meet her."
"I am taking it slow mother," he told her with an ironic smile. "I know it's unlike me but I think she might be the one."

"You think or you know?"

"I have never felt this way before and it is frustrating me to no end knowing that I am going to have to play by the rules," he said with a slow smile.

"Anything worth having is worth fighting for," she told him gently. She had been secretly waiting for this moment and now that it was here she was glad she was around to see it. "Why don't you invite her to dinner here?"

"I want to but I do not want to put any pressure on her. We talk a lot over the phone everyday but I still have to be cautious how I approach her with certain things." He put his hands behind his head and stared at the ceiling for a minute. "She is special and beautiful and sometimes she would stop in the middle of a conversation and grab a napkin and scribble something down as if inspiration had just struck and she would forget that I was there for a minute."

"It must be something new for you," she teased.

"It certainly is," he said with a slow smile. "She is something else and the funny thing about it is I am not interested in anyone else. Do you think it is the fun of the chase?"

"Are you doing any chasing?" his mother countered, one eyebrow raised.

"I am not," he admitted looking at her quizzically. "I am content to be what she wants now, is that weird?"

"No, you are taking a new direction or rather your heart is and your body is going along with it."

"That's one way to put it." He said with a smile.

"Get some sleep darling and don't worry about it." She leaned over to squeeze his hand gently before climbing off the bed. She stood there looking at the handsome lean muscular man she had borne inside her for nine months twenty-seven years ago and left the room hoping that he had finally found true love; it was about time for him.

Chapter 4

"How about a picnic?" she called him one day while he was in the middle of putting together some reports for his dad and the board. They had had their first court date just yesterday and it was going well.

"In the middle of October with all this rain?" he teased her. She was big on impulse and when she resurfaced from her writing she would suggest the craziest things. He had taken her out to dinner two more times and had not even gone inside her house but left her at the steps with a peck on the forehead.

"We could have it indoors," she said. "Come on it will be fun."

"When?"

"How about now?" she suggested.

"Kym it's not quite three o'clock and I have a board meeting in a few minutes."

"Oh," she sounded very disappointed. "Okay, how about later when you are off work?"

"I will leave straight from here and come," he told her wishing he could ditch the meeting and go to her but he did not want to seem to be too eager. "Want me to bring anything?"

"Just your fine self," she told him teasingly. "I have ordered a few things from the store in town and they do delivery so I am all set."

"Okay I will see you later."

*****

Kymonia peeked outside to see if Mrs. Willows was anywhere around. The woman had offered to make some cucumber sandwiches and some broccoli salad dip for her. It had stopped raining and the sun had come out but the chill was still there. She put on a sweater over her thin cotton blouse and headed over to her neighbor's house. "Mrs. Willows?" she pushed open the picket fence which had been slightly ajar and went on up to the cobbled steps. "Mrs. Willows?" she used the circular knocker.

"I am in the kitchen dear," the woman called out. Inside the house was so different from hers. There were colorful throw pillows all around and ever since she had retired she had started painting still life and the paintings were all around the cozy living room and the smell of baking permeated the room.

"Something smells wonderful," she said sniffing the air.

"I am making a pecan pie to go with the other things I am giving you," she said with a beaming smile. She had an apron around her narrow waist and a chef's hat on her white hair.

"You did not have to do that," Kymonia protested taking a seat on one of the stools around the counter.

"No problem my dear, I enjoy cooking for others." She said with a smile. "I want you to impress that young man of yours."

"It's not really like that," Kymonia told her reaching for a freshly baked cookie and tasting it; loving the texture and the lightness of it. "We are just friends for now."

"Oh pish posh," she snorted. "That young man is clearly taken with you and if you would only get your head out of that book of yours for a few minutes you would realize that I am telling you the truth."

"Even so I am not ready for that kind of commitment yet." She said firmly.

"Clifton and I were friends for a year before we started going out as a couple," she smiled as she remembered. She had taken out the delicious smelling pie from the oven and placed it on a cake plate to allow it to cool. "I was not sure we would make it as lovers but he insisted it could work and I ended up falling in love with him. He was my best friend and husband all rolled into one and he was the only man for me. The only regret we had was not being able to have children but we never let that bother us in the least or affect our relationship."

"That's so romantic," Kymonia mused. "It sounds like something I should be writing about."

"Or something you should be living," the woman told her wisely.

"It would not be fair to him," she said with a shrug, dusting off her hands to get rid of the cookie crumbs. "I'm in a cloud most times and sometimes it takes me days to surface. You know that because you have to come over to see if I am still alive."

"If you had someone I would not have to," Mrs. Willows looked at the beautiful girl in front of her curiously.

"Still would not be fair." She hopped off the stool. "All ready for me?"

"Of course my dear. I will just bag up everything and get them ready for you."

*****

He came by after six and what he did not tell her was that he had to put aside some things he had to do in order for him to be there on time. She had showered and put on faded denims and a red sweater and her hair was loose around her face. "I bought a bottle of Chardonnay after all," he said holding up the bottle. His hair was slightly damp from the rain that had come down suddenly and as soon as she took the wine from him he shrugged out of his jacket to reveal a powder blue shirt and red and blue tie which he pulled immediately. She led the way into the living room where there was a fire blazing in the hearth."Nice," he murmured noticing that she had already spread the blanket and there was a picnic basket in the middle.

"Shoes off please," she told him with an impish smile and he noticed that she was already barefooted. "I have no culinary skills whatsoever and since we are friends and there is really no need to impress you then I will tell you that the food or most of it is complimentary of my next door neighbor Mrs. Willows."

"I need to thank her," he murmured, trying not to notice her reference to them as only friends.

She sat and he followed suit while she reached inside the basket and came up with a variety of food. There were crispy fried chicken, two kinds of dip, sandwiches and a pecan pie that smelled heavenly. She shared a plate for him and then herself and they started eating.

"So what did you do today?" he asked her casually, biting into the chicken with relish.

"I wrote a little bit then I fell asleep watching a soap opera." She told him with a laugh. "I don't watch daytime television but I was a little fed up with writing so I decided to take a break."

"You have something on your chin," he reached over and used a napkin to wipe the piece of chicken from her skin and his eyes caught hers and held. He used the napkin to touch her cheek and ran it over her lips. His green eyes had darkened and his hand lingered against her lips.

"Julian," she murmured softly.

"I want to kiss you," he told her huskily.

"I want you to," she told him.

He leaned forward and she met him halfway. His mouth captured hers and she sank right into the kiss with a sigh and a whisper. His tongue entered her mouth tentatively as if waiting for some sign that she did not want him to and then ventured further as he realized that she was responding. Her hands lifted to touch his shoulders and his muscles flexed at the touch of her hands on him. His mouth moved over hers and he shuddered as the passion unleashed itself inside them. He broke away with a sigh and had to fight to regain control of his emotions. He looked at her and realized that her eyes were still closed as if waiting for him to continue.

"We are taking it slow remember?" he told her with a shaky laugh. "I don't want to ruin anything and have you telling me that I am still the same person who you have read about in the papers. I want to prove myself to you before we start another chapter Kym."

"And what is this other chapter going to be?" she asked him, trying to tamp down the desire that was racing through her.

"The chapter where we both want each other equally and everything is mutual."

She looked at him for a moment and then nodded, her long lashes shielding her eyes. "I have asked you before why you are doing this and you told me that you want to show me that you have changed. I keep telling myself that I am not interested in a relationship and I don't think I am but I like this," she gestured with her hands vaguely. "I like where we are at the moment and I kind of like you Julian."

"That's good to hear," he told her. "I more than like you."

*****

"Are you crazy?" Gabrielle stared at her friend in shock. "You have been going out with that totally handsome and rich guy and you have no idea what his penis looks like?"

"I appreciate your bluntness," Kym told her dryly.
They were having lunch at a restaurant downtown. It had been a week since the picnic at her house and he had called her

Page 70

every day to make sure she was okay; he was definitely growing on her. The weather had turned wretchedly cold and it almost felt like winter although it was just autumn.

"I side with Gabby on this one." Marla was dressed in a bulky green sweater and purple stretch pants and was wearing a black wig with purple strands. "What kind of a strange relationship do you two have going on?"

"We are friends," Kym told them defensively.

"How can you not want to have sex with him? He is every woman's dream! What's wrong with you?" Gabrielle asked her.

"I am taking it slow and he does not mind it one bit," Kym dug her fork into her fries smothered with ketchup and refused to rise to their bait.

"Are you sure about that?" Gabrielle asked her eyebrows rose. She had come off her diet and was having the beef soup with everything in it.

"We talk about stuff so I am sure he would tell me if he has some reservations." Kym said with a shrug.

"You live in a world all your own honey," Marla said with a shake of her head. "He is a man and that's saying one thing: sex is totally on his mind."

*****

Kymonia took the cup of tea and went outside on her balcony. It was cold but she had bundled up in her special thick blanket and ventured out to sit on the porch swing she had had installed a few months ago.

It was almost seven and the time had gotten dark a long time ago. She could see the glare from the streetlights on the main road and the leaves shivering in the wind that was blowing. She could also see that Mrs. Willows was in her living room probably painting something, maybe some fruits or a flower.

It was so peaceful and quiet and lonely, her mind whispered. She looked around startled as if expecting to see someone else besides her on the porch. She had never felt lonely before because she had always been comfortable with her own company and she usually had her writing to involve herself in. What brought this on? She wondered. She had spoken to Julian earlier and he had told her he was on his way home and had told her to eat something which she had done so. But she wanted to hear his voice again before she turned in for the night. She reached for her cell phone before she could change her mind and dialed his number.

He answered immediately. "Hey," his deep voice sounded in her ear.

"Are you home?" she asked him.

"Just got in not too long ago," he answered and she just wanted to keep on hearing his voice. "What no writing tonight?" he teased her.

"No, taking the night off and watching the wind move the leaves on the trees and enjoying some lemon tea." She told him softly. "I just wanted to say hey."

"You sure you are okay?" he wanted her to say no and he wished she would.

"I guess. I was just feeling a little bit lonely and morbid. I am trying to find stories everywhere but I am going to go to bed now. How about you?" she asked him.

"I have some things to do before I do then it's off to bed for me as well." He paused. "Are you sure you are okay?"

"Hmm," she sipped the tea and stood up hugging the robe closer to her. "I am now; it was good talking to you."

"Anytime," he told her softly. "How about taking in a movie tomorrow?"

"Sounds good." She said with a smile in her voice.

"Good night Kym,"

"Good night Julian," she hung up the phone and went inside her bedroom. She had almost asked him to come over but that would not have been fair to him and she had no intention of using him just because of how she felt at a particular time. With a sigh she removed the comforter and slipped underneath.

That night she dreamt that he was beside her holding her close and telling her that he was never going to leave.

*****

Julian pulled the shirt over his head and stared at himself in the bathroom mirror. She had called him and it had not been something he had initiated. He had wanted so much to go over to her place and hold her in his arms but he had to let her make the first move which she was not doing. But she had called and that was something.

He sighed and straightened up. He had been about to take a shower when she called and now the sound of her voice had done something to him, he doubt he would be able to go to sleep right now, he thought ruefully. He was going to be thinking about her a lot tonight.

*****

They went to watch a romantic comedy. He picked her up at eight dressed in denims and a dark green sweater that matched his eyes. She had chosen to wear a long black wool skirt and black and white sweater and long boots and she had put her hair into a ponytail.

"You look beautiful," he told her as soon as she opened the door.

"Thanks, you don't look too bad yourself," she told him with a smile. "Are we late?"

"Not quite, why?" he asked her as he came further inside the room.

"I need to jot down something that came to mind just as you knocked on the door." She told him.

"Go ahead." He suggested. "I will just sit here and watch something on television."

"Don't be silly!" she exclaimed reaching for his hand and pulling him with her towards the office. "I want to show you where I work."

She led him into the small but neat office where she went behind her desk and booted up her computer. "I have notepads everywhere in the house including the bathroom," she grinned. "You never know when inspiration will strike."

"I see," he wandered around the room and took in the bookcase stocked with books of all sort and the colorful curtains at the large bay windows that looked out on the rolling hills and a glimpse of what looked like an old abandoned house.

She was hard at work and he watched her as she focused on the computer screen at what she was typing, her smooth brow knit somewhat into a slight frown of concentration. She had a mini fridge inside the room as well as cozy sofa where he suspected she slept sometimes when she worked late.

"Okay done," she told him brightly, saving her work and shutting down. "Thanks for understanding." She walked over to him and to his surprise she came straight into his arms, putting her hands around his neck. "My friends think I am an idiot." She murmured.

"Why would they think that?" he asked her huskily, closing his hands around her small waist.

"Because we have not been to bed yet." She told him honestly watching his eyes narrow. "They think I am out of my mind."

"Are you?" he murmured his eyes on her full lips that had on a peach lip gloss that highlighted the shape of her lips.

"What do you think?" she asked him standing on her toes to touch his lips with hers.

"I disagree," he took her lips with his with a groan. She opened her mouth underneath his, feeling the thundering of her heart and the shaking of her body. His tongue delved inside her mouth and his arms tightened around her body as he deepened the kiss. Kym wanted to just put aside her reservations and let him take her into the bedroom, she wished she could but she was determined that she was not going to be another one of his women, the ones that fall so easily to his charms. He had been showing her that he had changed but she was still cautious and a little afraid because she had started to think of him as more than a friend.

He pulled away from her abruptly, his breathing ragged. "If we continue we are not going to make the movies," he told her hoarsely, his hands clenched into fists. "Shall we," he indicated the doorway.

Kym looked at him for a moment also fighting for control then she nodded and preceded him from the room. They were quiet on their way to the theater, each immersed in their own thoughts.

He opened the door for her to get out and handed the keys to the valet. The wind had picked up somewhat and he pulled her closer to him, his arms around her and he did not let go until they were in the movie theater. He bought her a huge bucket of popcorn and she curled up against him ready to enjoy the show.

"I love romantic comedies," she whispered after awhile. "I get ideas for my books when I watch them sometimes."

Her body beside his and so close was affecting him more than he wanted to admit. The kiss they had shared inside her home office had not worn off one bit and he wanted to pull her onto his lap and devoured her right here and now. "A true writer," he forced himself to say lightly.

Kym angled her head up to his and stared at his handsome profile. "You have never been friends with a woman before have you?"

"Not since kindergarten," he told her with a short laugh. "This is a first for me but I can handle it or at least I think I can."

She reached for his hand and linked it with hers. "I think a relationship that starts with friendship first lasts the longest." She murmured, her dark brown eyes meeting his.

"What are you saying?" he asked her hoarsely, his hand tightening on hers.

"I think this is the beginning of something special," she told him softly.

He bent his head and took her lips hungrily, his hand gripping the back of her neck as he pulled her into the kiss. Kym shuddered against him, moaning inside his mouth as her hands crept up and tightened on his sweater, holding on for leverage. His mouth moved over hers, his tongue seeking hers and finding her as she opened up to him. His pulse was racing! And he felt the control slipping away from him as her soft lips drove him crazy with need. He had to get them out of here, one part of his mind thought fighting the fog that was covering his brain. He had to get them out before they were charge for indecent exposure.

"We have to go," he dragged his mouth from hers and rested his forehead against hers, trying to control his breathing.

"I agree," she told him, her fists still bunched inside his sweater.

They left immediately, almost with indecent haste. He could feel his erection burning a hole in his pants as he pulled away from the building. He did not say anything to her, he couldn't and he kept as far away as possible from her as could happen in the confines of the vehicle.

He pulled up outside her gate and his hands clenched on the wheel, his eyes closed.

"Aren't you coming in?" she asked him quietly. He turned to look at her, his green eyes narrowed as he took in her mouth still swollen from his kiss, his body shivering at what she was not saying.

"Are you sure?" he said hoarsely.

"Yes, I won't get any sleep tonight if you leave."

Chapter 5

He followed behind her when they left the car and watched impatiently while she used the key to open the door. He did not want to appear too desperate but as soon as they were inside he pulled her up against him. "I am sorry," he muttered. "I wanted this to be special and romantic but I can't wait."

"Neither can I," she told him reaching up to cup his face in her hands before dragging his head down towards hers.

With a groan he lifted her up against him and took her to one of the bedrooms and pushed open the door. He placed her on the bed and undressed her slowly, staring at every inch of bare skin that was revealed as the layer of her clothes was removed. She was beautiful! He thought, his hands spanning her small waist. He stepped back and removed his clothing climbing on the bed beside her.

His muscles rippled and she noticed that he was tanned all over. He was magnificent! And she could see why women allowed him to do whatever he wanted with them. There was a smattering of dark hair on his chest and she splayed her hands on his chest.

He bent his head and took her lips with his. Kym reached up and put her hands around his neck pulling him closer to her, his chest hair rubbing against her nipples and causing them to harden even further. He reached a hand between their bodies and felt for her, his hand touching her pubic area, touching her mound. She gasped softly and arched her body against his. He dipped a finger inside her as his mouth moved over hers insistently and Kym felt the passion raging through her as his fingers thrust inside her.

He released her mouth and went down to capture her nipple between his teeth, his tongue caressing her as his teeth grazed the flesh. She gasped and gripped his head, her fingers pulling at his hair. He moved over to her other nipple and by this time she was shivering uncontrollably.

"Julian," she whispered.

He lifted his head and stared at her, his green eyes darkened. He moved over her and gently entered her, his eyes still on hers. Her tightness enclosed him like a glove and he shuddered as he pushed himself further inside her. She opened up for him like a flower receiving nectar and with a tortured groan he started moving inside her, his teeth clenched.

His thrusting became more frantic and hurried as she moved underneath him, her hands clasped around his neck, her body in sync with his. He felt the pressure building up inside him and he knew he was not going to last very long. He pulled out of her for a little bit, his breathing ragged as he tried to fight the raging passion inside him. He had never felt this way before and it was something he had to get used to.

He rubbed the tip of his penis on her mound and looked with narrowed eyes as her lips parted and she gasped. He entered her again, this time forcefully, his hands gripping her hips, bringing her closer to him. He felt his penis burgeoning inside the walls of her vagina and filled her up so much that he thought he would burst with the pressure of it.

She met his thrusts with hers and he felt her nipples brushing against his chest. He felt her body shuddering and knew what was coming next because he felt it within him as well. With a groan he took her lips as the cry tore from her throat combined with his hoarse calling of her name as the orgasm crashed over them like a wave!

She clung to him as he moved inside her still. His mouth was still on hers and she felt the passion racing through her body. She never dreamed she could feel so much emotion clamoring for supremacy in her body. She had never felt this way before and it frightened her that he could make her feel like this. He had not used protection but she had been on the pills for years now to regulate her periods so she was safe and she was not even thinking about that when he had kissed her in the movie theater. That had been the farthest thing from her mind. His touch had driven every sensible thought out of her mind and all she had wanted was to be with him.

He released her lips and rested his forehead against hers. "I want to stay tonight." He murmured, his breath fanning her face.

"I want that as well," she told him and with a sigh he took her lips with his again.

*****

He did not allow her to sleep. He kept her awake while his mouth searched every inch of her body, using his tongue to lick and tease and titillate. Kym was kept in constant need as he took her to heights she had never dreamt possible. When his mouth went down on her she cried out sharply and as his tongue entered her she came inside his mouth, sobbing as the feelings wracked her body with a force that was overwhelming.

He finally allowed her to sleep but even so he kept his hand on her pubic area as he watched her fall into an exhausted sleep, her mouth slightly opened. She was beautiful! He thought and not for the first time, his eyes wandering over her face and the full breasts bare and opened to his gaze. There was no one to compare to her and for the first time in his life someone meant something more than a roll in the hay and someone to slake his thirst whenever the need arose. He was falling in love with her and it was taking some getting used to.

*****

He spent the night and left late the next morning, waking her up with his mouth on her nipples. It was almost ten o'clock before they got out of bed and she found some milk and eggs and made them omelets and coffee with some fruits before he told her that he had to go into the office and he was already late for a meeting. It was Friday and she had some writing to do and some grocery shopping to do.

"Will I see you later?" she asked him as he got ready to leave.

"I will call you," he took her into his arms and kissed her gently on the lips before he left.

*****

"Hi Kym, how lovely to see you," Tyrone the local grocer hailed her as she went into the building. "You finally surfaced from that laptop of yours." He beamed as he came over and took her to show her some fresh produce that just came in. He was a middle aged African American who had taken over from his father when he died several years ago and had added a fresh produce area to the supermarket.

She noticed that there were few people walking around and taking up foodstuff. It was a small town and that was one of the reasons she had bought her house here. She knew most of the locals and they were always chatting her up, never really impressed by her so called fame.

"Hi Mrs. Bingham," she said waving to the elderly woman who was leaning on her cane and examining a cantaloupe closely. "How are you?"

"I am well my dear," the woman beamed waving back. She greeted a few others before picking up some fresh vegetables and fruits. She mostly ate on the go and cooking was not her thing but she always liked to have something in the pantry as well as in her food basket.

Tyrone handed her a large watermelon as soon as she came to cash her items. "Compliments of the greenhouse," he beamed as he rang up her sale.

"Oh Tyrone thanks," she said in genuine delight. "I had no idea they had started bearing already."

"It was due to the showers of rain we have been receiving." He told her with a smile. "Going back to your writing now?"

"I am planning on doing that but I am supposed to go and meet with my editor as well." Kym told him taking up the bag with her items neatly packed.

"Ah the life of an artist." He said with a sigh as he handed her back her card. "Did I tell you that when I was a kid I wanted to be a writer?" he asked her probably for the fourth time. "But I just could not get my words right, so now I create art in my greenhouse," he said giving her a white grin that crinkled his dark brown eyes.

"Art is art," Kymonia told him with a smile and left.

She drove home and put away the items she had bought and quickly changed into dark blue dress pants and a blue and white silk shirt, brushing out her hair and applying make-up sparingly. It was a little past two and she had a three o'clock appointment with her editor.

All through the day she had tried not to let it bother her that she had not heard from Julian all day. At other times, he would be calling her to check up on her and to find out whether or not she had eaten and how her writing was progressing but today she had not heard from him. What if he had gotten what he wanted so he had no need to call her again? Something whispered in her mind.

With a feeling of determination she shook it off and got ready to leave the house.

"Kymonia," Mrs. Willows called out to her just as she was about to hop into her car.

"Mrs. Willows, I am sorry. I am running a little late for my meeting." She had donned her tan cashmere coat because it had been chilly when she went out earlier.

"I saw you going out this morning and I wanted you to pick up some fresh milk for me," the woman said apologetically. "I am afraid I overslept this morning because I was up a bit late last night doing some painting." Kym felt a moment of relief on hearing that she had slept late and therefore had not seen Julian leave this morning.

"I will pick them up on the way back." She assured her before getting in the car.

*****

"You look different," were the first words out of Sylvia's mouth as soon as she stepped inside her office. The publishing house was located a little distance from where she lived and it had taken her an hour to get there and all the time in the car she had been expecting to hear from Julian so by the time she reached the publishing house she was a mass of nerves.

"No I don't; it's your imagination." Kym took a seat in front of the woman's crowded desk and wondered as she always did how she managed to get any work done.

"I am sure it's not because you are the one with the imagination." The woman continued to look at her closely, her red painted lips pursed in concentration. Kym felt as if she was under a microscope or in the principal's office.

"Are we having this meeting or not?" she asked the woman coolly.

"Always in a hurry," Sylvia said shaking her bottled blonde curls. She had a red silk blouse that did not quite fit her very ample bosom very well and the make-up was heavy on her florid face.

"I made some changes to chapter two," she saw the expression on the young woman's face and said hurriedly. "Just something slight darling," she assured her. "I think Katherine should have a heated argument with Tony and leave the room in a blaze of anger."

Kym studied the changes and made some of her own passing them to Sylvia. "Excellent darling," the woman said with a pleased smile. "I also have your royalty check for the month right here." She passed an envelope to Kym. "Open it," she urged.

Kym did so and her eyes widened as she saw the amount of zeroes there. "What happened?"

"An increase in sales darling." Sylvia told her with a smile. "There is one tiny problem though,"

"What is it?" Kym asked dragging her eyes away from the check in her hand.

"Your readers are clamoring for your story."

"What do you mean my story?" Kym looked at her puzzled.

"You don't seem to have an active love life and yet you are writing romance novels that sizzle the pages of your book. People want to know that you have at least a man that is servicing you on a regular basis."

Kym grimaced at her choice of words. "That's none of their damned business."

"We both know that's not true." Sylvia told her mildly. "You are an exceptionally beautiful woman who happens to write some of the best love scenes I have ever read, they want to know that the inspiration is not plucked from thin air."

"So my imagination as a writer does not count for anything?" she asked heatedly.

"Of course it does darling, but it's not enough. They need to know that a man is in the picture as well." Sylvia told her. "You are a public figure and therefore your business is open to all and sundry and your readers want to know that the person they admire so much is also real and capable of those very feeling she portrays in her books. Get yourself a man honey and make those pages sizzle even more."

*****

Julian let the meeting wash over him without paying any attention to what they were saying. He had not lied to her when he had told her he had meetings to attend. He had done the status report for the building he had seen and was interested in and they had discussed it at the board level.

He was not doing well. He had picked up the phone to call her several times but he had not done so, he had a lot of thinking to do. He had made love to her over and over again and he had found that the more he had her, the more he wanted her. She was under his skin and in his blood and he was not used to a woman having so much power over him. He felt trapped and scared and what was worse he was falling in love with her!

*****

Kym felt the anger gathering inside her and festering. She had left the publishing house with a deceptive calmness about her and had climbed inside her car and closed the door against the cold wind whipping at her coat. It had rained last night and the water was still settled on the pavement.

He still had not called her and she felt the bitter disappointment going through her. He had slept with her and was done with her and she had allowed him to do so. She had become another notch on his belt and she had sworn that she would never be.

She pushed the button to start the car and drove off determined not to cry, she bit her lip and concentrated on the road.

*****

She had a late lunch with the girls. Gabrielle was just coming out of court and Marla had just finished dropping off some outfits she had for a store downtown so they met in a fast food restaurant.

Kym ordered a small salad and fruit punch while her friends ordered fried chicken and coleslaw. "On a diet?" Marla asked her tapered brows raised in question.

"No appetite," Kym responded. "I slept with Julian last night." She added abruptly. "Not that we did much sleeping."

"Girl, that's wonderful!" Gabrielle exclaimed biting into her succulent chicken.

"Finally, this calls for a toast." Marla said with a grin.

"He has not called me since." She told them, her expression woebegone.

"The man just left this morning, give him some time." Marla told her.

"He usually calls me at least three times a day to check up on me and now that we have progressed to the next stage he has not done so. What does that say?"

"That maybe he is busy and has not gotten around to doing so yet?" Gabrielle suggested.

"I don't believe that," Kym said shaking her head. "No matter how busy he was in the past he always called and now when I have given him you know what; I do not hear from him."

"You know honey, I am going to ask you one question," Gabrielle said. "Was it good?"

"It was mind blowing good." Kym admitted crunching on her salad.

"It works both ways. You had pleasure in the highest form and you enjoyed each other's company immensely. If he does not call you back then you look back on what you shared with a smile and move on knowing that you had a grand experience."

"Easy for you to say," Kym muttered.

"It's not and I have reached a point in my life where I am not going to get hung up on the pressure of expecting to be called after I have been with a man, it calls of too much heartbreak and complications."

*****

She picked up several cartons of milk on her way back home for Mrs. Willows and decided to stay a little bit after dropping them off.

"How about some of my famous pot pie?" She asked as soon as Kym came inside the warm and cozy living room.

"You know I cannot say no to your cooking," she smiled and followed her to the kitchen.

It was a little after five and she had given up hearing from Julian. Gabrielle was right; it was just going to be a very pleasant memory for her.

Mrs. Willows put the steaming plate in front of her and Kym sniffed the steam rising from it appreciatively. "Mom tried to teach me the art of cooking but I was always wrapped up in some book or the other and never willing to learn. One

Thanksgiving I tried to bake the turkey but got lost inside a book I was reading and I almost burned the kitchen down." She laughed softly at the memory. "Mom made me promise never to go inside the kitchen again."

"I always loved to cook," Mrs. Willows said with a smile."I was into experimenting and would make my poor husband be my guinea pig. He would taste whatever I asked him to without complaining until I perfected the art of whatever it was I was making. I find cooking to be therapeutic and I think it's one of those things that has kept me over the years after my husband passed away, that and my painting."

They ate in silence for a little bit then the woman surprised her by saying: "Quite a handsome young man you got yourself there last night," her watery blue eyes looked at the beautiful young girl curiously.

"You saw him?" Kym asked her resignedly.

"Of course, I always look out to make sure you are not being abducted or anything like that," the woman told her mildly. "It looks serious."

"It's not," Kym told her firmly spooning the liquid and vegetables into her mouth and wishing she did not have to talk about it. "He has not called."

"And you are not going to call him of course because that would be too forward of you." Mrs. Willows said shrewdly. "It's funny how we have come so far where technology is concerned and yet we are still mired in the past. In my days it would be considered a mortal sin if a woman contacted a man first but nowadays it is supposed to be acceptable." She paused and looked at Kym. "I have a feeling that that young man is probably waiting to hear from you as well my dear and probably just as confused as you are."

"I strongly doubt that," Kym said dryly. "He is rich and handsome and is used to getting his own way so there is no way he is shy about calling. If he has not called it means he has lost interest."

"He has been showing interest all along, why should he be lacking in interest now?"

"Because I foolishly allowed him to get what he wanted and now he is no longer interested!" Kym said bitterly.

Chapter 6

Three days passed and he did not call. She immersed herself in her writing with a vengeance. Her mother called and spoke to her about a neighbor dying.

"He was not sick dear and I realized I had not seen him in several days." Her mother told her, voice subdued. "They found him dead inside the house."

"I am sorry to hear that mom," she said sympathetically, looking at what she had written so far. "Didn't he have any children?"

"Just a son, his wife died fifteen years ago and the son did not really come around."

"How are you taking it?" Kym asked her in concern.

"I am just realizing more than ever how short life is." She murmured. "How are you dear?"

"I am just trying to get this book finished so I can take a little break. I am thinking of maybe going to Europe for a little bit."

"Honey are you sure you are okay? What is this about going to Europe?"

"I need to go away and forget about writing for a bit." She told her.

"I hope you know you can talk to me about anything honey." Her mother told her.

"I know mom," she told her fondly. "Tell pops hi for me."

"I will dear."

*****

He called her on the third day and she looked at the number and his name and did not answer the phone. He kept calling her throughout the day but she turned off her phone and continued writing.

The day had turned out quite well, not so cold and with a bright sun shining from the still leaden sky. She decided that she should go out to the abandon building and see if inspiration would hit. Packing a picnic basket with some fruits and cheese sandwiches and a bottle of white wine that had been chilling in the fridge. Putting on her poncho and old jeans, she went on her way.

The roof of the building was still intact and the walls were still solid but the floors had crumbled in places. It had originally been a manor and the columns were still majestic and towered in the air. She had explored the rooms and tried to imagine what it had been like living in the house. There were numerous bedrooms and there was a huge fireplace in the hall, large enough to be used as a room. She closed her eyes and pictured the occupants of the house. She had done her research and knew that it had been in one family for six generations until the current owner had abandoned the huge house and gone away leaving it to crumble. It still had not lost its grandeur. She had planned to base a novel in this very spot and she had even gotten pictures of its former glory and was going to write something about a renaissance romance.

She spread the blanket and took out the food she had taken with her and started to eat feeling the cold coming through the thick poncho but she wanted to be outside for a little bit and away from her house. She needed time to think and not about what she had shared with Julian. She had felt something for him and when they had made love that feeling had spiraled above anything she had ever experienced before.

She had finished eating and was lying on her back with her hands behind her head when she heard footsteps on the uneven floor. Before she turned her head to look she knew it was him because her body had tightened in awareness. He stopped within a few inches away from her. "Your very nice and nosy neighbor told me you might be here," he told her softly.

Her eyes traveled the length of him from his black leather boots to his black dress pants and up to his green ribbed sweater that matched his eyes perfectly. His hair was tousled and made him look boyishly handsome and as she looked at his lips, she remembered his mouth all over her body. "I come here sometimes to get inspiration and imagine what the former occupants of this place felt like living here. The architecture is still beautiful and those columns are magnificent." She pointed to them.

He crouched down beside her, knowing from her tone that he was going to have a hell of a time convincing her that him not calling her was unlike his usual modus operandi. "I needed time to think about what I feel when I am with you." He ventured.

"Don't worry about it," she told him getting up and pulling her knees under her chin, her dark brown eyes cool and indifferent. "We had a good time so let's leave it at that. How are you?"

She was polite and indifferent and she was looking straight through him. He had left it too long. "Terrible," he told her forcing himself to remain calm. "I have not been able to sleep and eat because I have been thinking about you so much."

"You'll get over it," she got up and started gathering her stuff together and he bent to help her, his heart thudding inside his chest. He was not getting through to her.

"I don't want to get over of it," he told her tightly holding on to the blanket as she reached for it. She let it go and held the picnic basket in her hand and started to walk away. "I am falling in love with you dammit!"

She stopped so suddenly that he almost careened into her. She turned around to face him and to his surprise she started to laugh. "You don't know what love is Julian," she told him coolly when she had finished laughing. "You probably think that I am gullible enough to believe you and that is a way of getting me back in bed. You do not have to go to such lengths, as I said we had a good time and if and when I want to do it again I will let you know."

She turned and started walking without waiting for what he had to say. He knew he deserved every damning word that came out of her mouth but he had no idea he could feel so much pain. He caught up to her and grabbed her arm forcing her to stop. "I tell you I am falling in love with you and you behave as if I just told you I found a beetle on the ground!" he took a deep breath to calm himself down before he continued. "I am not an imbecile Kym! I know I don't have the best reputation but I know what I feel! I was scared and I hid because I've never felt this way before and I was thinking that you have way too much power over me, I did not know what to do."

"You don't owe me an explanation," she told him coldly trying to pull her arm away from him but he held on. "You are not capable of being in a committed relationship and I get that but don't come here and try to convince me that you have changed, you are who you are and you cannot change that."

He wanted to shake her until he saw the fire in her eyes and he wanted to stop the despair from drowning him. "I changed when I met you," his voice sounded weary and her heart almost, but not quite, went out to him, she could not afford to drop her guard again. "I saw you that night at the bar and I have not been able to be with anyone else since. I know what I feel and I am asking you to give me a chance." His eyes had turned bleak as he looked down at her. The wind had whipped her curls around her exquisite face and even though her face was devoid of make-up she looked wonderful. "I have never begged for anything in my life but I am begging you to give me a chance."

She stood there staring up at him and she wanted to throw her hands around his neck and sink into him but she stood her ground. "I don't want you to beg." She told him quietly. "I just want to be left alone and continue the way I was before, I cannot handle a relationship right now anyway."

"If you can look at me and tell me that you did not feel something when we made love then I will walk away from you, as difficult as it may be," his tone was quiet and his grip had loosened a little.

"I can't tell you that," she looked up at him and suddenly she wanted to touch him, touch his face and soothe away the lines of misery she saw there. "I felt something when we were together but you went away and did not call and that killed it and it's not something I want to rekindle."

"No!" the word tore from his mouth and to her surprise he pulled her into his arms. She dropped the basket as he hauled her close to him and before she could stop him, his mouth took hers savagely, his movements desperate. She clung to him and her mouth opened underneath his unconsciously. His arms came around her like a vice and he deepened the kiss, his mouth moving over hers, his hands roaming over her body as if seeking some sort of solace for the pain he was feeling.

He broke away from her after a few minutes, his fists clenched at his sides. "Please," he whispered hoarsely.

Kym was shaken badly and she felt the blood coursing through her veins. She knew without a doubt that she was far from indifferent to him. "I can't," she whispered but she knew she was weakening.

"You can," his voice was urgent. The wind was blowing around them and the place had gotten dark. It was cold but they did not notice, neither of them felt the cold nipping at their clothes. Her eyes widened as he went down on one knee in front of her. "I want to marry you; will you do me the honor of becoming my wife?"

Kym stood there looking down at him, her dark brown eyes wide. "Julian, what are you doing?"

"I can't see my life without you; I spent three days trying to see if I could and I discovered that I am miserable and lost without you." He paused. "I want you to be my wife; you don't have to change your lifestyle and I will give you space to exercise your creativity. I won't interfere but just give me this."

"We don't know anything about each other-" she did not get a chance to continue.

"We can change that, please say yes." He stood up and took her hands in his, looking down at her. "I need you in my life; I don't want to be without you."

"I need time," She told him slowly, her head spinning.

"I will give you three days," he smiled at her grimly. "The same time it took to get my head on straight and stop running away from my feelings. How is that?"

She nodded. "Are you sure?" she asked him.

"Sure about giving you the three days?" he asked her grimly. "No, because it means that I am not going to be able to function while I am waiting for your answer. Have I mentioned that I have never been in this position before?"

"I mean are you sure about wanting to marry me?" she corrected.

"I have never been so sure about anything in my life." He told her softly. "I want to kiss you but I am afraid if I start it will lead to me taking you right here, that's how much I want you."

She moved closer to him, her heart pounding. "I want you to," she whispered her arms going around his neck.

With a groan he lifted her up and carried her the short distance to the house.

*****

He called her every day and did not mention the offer he had made her. They had made love desperately and with so much emotion that it had left them trembling in its wake. He had not left there until the morning and only because he said he wanted to give her space to make up her mind.

Kym could not think of anything else. He wanted to marry her and she did not know what she wanted. When she was with him she did not want him to leave and he made her feel as if her body was on fire and only he had the remedy for what was happening to her.

She had not told her parents about him yet and she was not sure what to tell them.

It was Friday and October was almost at an end. The cloud was leaden and heavy and the morning was very cold. She was supposed to give her answer to Julian tomorrow and she was still thinking about it.

"You look serious," Gabrielle commented as soon as she opened the door to let them in.

She did not have court today and had taken the day off to deal with some personal matters when Kym had called her and asked her to come over.

"What's wrong?" Marla asked shrugging out of her bright orange fall coat.

"Can we at least sit first before I start?" Kym asked walking into the living room. "Julian asked me to marry me." She told them abruptly.

There was silence for a while as both girls stared at her.

"That's the same reaction I had when he asked me." She told them wryly.

"What did you tell him?" Marla asked her quietly.

"I told him I needed time and my time is up tomorrow." She said with a sigh leaning back against the sofa.

"Why is it so hard to say yes?" Gabrielle asked her. "Are you in love with him?"

"That's it," Kym spread her hands helplessly. "I know when I am with him I feel as if my body is on fire but I love this," she gestured around the place. "I love being on my own and doing my own thing. You know how I am sometimes when the bug hits me and I start writing; I go for days on end without talking to anyone and barely going to the bathroom or even to eat. What am I going to do with a husband?"

"Honey, does he know your habits?" Gabrielle asked her.

"He does, at least some of it."

"Then you need to tell him the rest of it and let him decide whether or not he can deal with that aspect of your life."

"What if he can't?" Kym stood up and started pacing restlessly.

"Then I am sure he will let you know." Marla told her. "From what you tell us, the man is in love with you and he is willing to try so it's up to you."

*****

He did not call her and she knew he was waiting on her to call him. She had got up early in the morning and despite the cold had bundled up in a thick blanket and gone on the porch with a cup of tea in her hand, still in her pajamas. She had spent the night staring up at the ceiling and thinking. She would never be a traditional wife that much she knew and even though she fancied herself married one day she knew she was too much of an independent and was too single minded to be thinking about another person. Sometimes she did not even think about herself.

She was also not prepared to give up her house, it was her solace and she had invested a lot of time and money into the place to let it go like that. On the other hand she loved how he made her feel and she did not want to lose that. She could talk to him about anything and he made her laugh and when he made love to her she did not want him to stop. But was that enough? She wondered, sipping the hot liquid thoughtfully. Was it enough to give up her freedom for?

*****

Julian prowled the length of his room as he waited for her to call. It was still early; a glance at the clock on the wall showed that it was only a little after eight but he had been up since four telling himself that if she said no he would just have to go on without her but he did not want to even think about that aspect of it.

He turned around as he heard a knock on his door. His father came inside and closed the door behind him. "You are going to wear out the carpet," he told him mildly, taking a seat on one of the plump and comfortable sofas in the room. "Your mother wants to know if you will be joining us for breakfast this morning."

"I am not hungry," he said abruptly. He knew he looked a sight because he had spent the morning plowing through his dark hair and his green eyes looked bleak.

"Is it the same young lady? The author?" James Robinson asked him.

"I asked her to marry me and I am still waiting on her answer." Julian said with a sigh as he came and sat beside his father. "I messed up when I slept with her and stayed away for three days and now it looks like she does not want to marry me. What am I going to do?"

"The day is far from over son." James said with a small lifting of his lips. He had never seen his usually confident and carefree son like this and it was good to know that someone had finally clipped his wings. "Give her some time."

"I am trying Dad but I am getting jumpy as hell," he admitted with a short laugh.

"I am sure she is worth the wait and the anticipation." He said with a pat on his son's hand. "Come on down after she has called and give us the good news."

*****

She called shortly after his father left the room and Julian snatched up the phone answering immediately not caring how desperate he seemed.

"I have thought about it and if you are willing to put up with my temperamental moods then the answer is yes, I will marry you." Her voice was soft and subdued.

"I want to ask you if you are sure but I am not going to take the chance that you might change your mind." He told her hoarsely, his shoulders sagging with relief. "I will put up with anything as long as you are with me."

"Okay then it's settled, are you coming over?" she asked him with laughter in her voice.

"My parents want to meet you. I will come over and then we come back here for dinner. "How does that sound?" he asked her quickly.

"Sounds good, I will be waiting." She said before disconnecting the call.

He sank back against the sofa the phone still in his hands and closed his eyes with immense relief. She had not said she loved him or anything like that but that could come after. She wanted to be his wife and that was all that mattered!

*****

She met his parents and was surprised to see how much like his father he looked. The house was a veritable mansion. Kym found herself looking at the large columns and structure of the place and the fountain in the middle of what looked like a special rose garden. The driveway was sweeping and circular and the grounds well kept and manicured.

"I have always admired you as an author my dear but the photo on the back cover of your books do you no justice." Irene Robinson told her with a smile. They were in the large elegant living room where there was a fire burning in the hearth and a uniformed maid had served them refreshments.

"Thank you," she smiled a little demurely, slightly intimidated by her sumptuous surroundings.

"My wife has been looking forward to your coming over so much that she has been looking out the window every few minutes." James Robinson told her with a teasing smile as he looked at his wife.

"James!" she exclaimed touching her husband lightly on the thigh. It struck Kym that their body language was one of a comfortable love that had blossomed and mellowed over the years. "It's true of course; I am after all, a fan."

She liked them, and she told Julian so when they were alone as he was showing her around.

"I am glad," he told her softly pulling her into his arms.

Chapter 7

He met her parents on Sunday. Gloria Rollins welcomed him with open arms and plied him with food and her stepfather Daniel insisted on showing him the garden even though it was drizzling and the afternoon was cold.

"You did not tell us you were seeing anyone let alone getting engaged dear, why the secrecy?" her mother asked as soon as the two men had left the room. Kym was helping her to clean up the leftovers from the meal they had just partaken and putting the dishes into the dishwasher.

"Because I wanted to be sure before I introduced him to you," she told her with a shrug. She had spent a wonderful time at his parents yesterday and had found herself warming up to them as the evening wore on.

"That young man is quite taken with you." She commented. "I see him looking at you when he knows you are not looking but I wonder if you feel the same way about him."

She stopped loading the dishes and looked at her mother. "I am attracted to him and I want to be with him but I am concerned about the fact that I am not your typical wife and I don't want to shortchange him."

"Loving someone means making some sort of a compromise my dear and I think he will do anything to make sure you are comfortable." She looked at her daughter for a moment. "It also means that you have to do some adjusting as well."

*****

He gave her a ring on Monday when he came over. He had spent the night with her on Sunday and left from her house to the office. It was a Princess cut diamond set against a platinum background and it fit her finger perfectly.

"Do you like it?" he asked her anxiously. He had spent the entire afternoon calling all the jewelry stores he knew and had found one in a small jewelry store uptown.

"It's beautiful," She murmured twisting her hand this way and that and watched as the lights from the lamp caught the stones and sent off a dazzling array of white blue glare.

"How about a December wedding?" she asked him. They were on the balcony even though it was quite cold. She had provided a thick blanket to cover them both and she was in his arms.

"Sound very good, are you sure that gives us enough time to plan?" he asked her.
"Us?" she turned her head to look at him. "Men are not usually involved in the planning."

"This man will be," he bent his head and took her lips with his, moving his mouth over hers in a slow and drugging kiss that had her heart racing. "I am going to show you that I have changed."

*****

He was true to his word. He told her that there were too many people around to help with the planning and he had also hired a wedding planner who along with his mother and hers took charge of everything.

They made the papers. Two very public people getting engaged was big news and the caption read: 'Romance writer Kymonia Blake finally injecting some romance into her life with none other than handsome billionaire playboy, Julian Robinson'.

Her editor called her and offered her congratulations. "Your readers are going crazy over this twist of romance in your life darling, brilliant move."

As the day approached, she started spending a few nights at Julian's place but she found that no matter what she did she was not able to write a single line. Mostly because he distracted her with his very presence and as much as he wanted to leave her to her writing he ended up coming into the office where he would kiss her neck and then it would lead to other things.

"I can't write when you are around Julian," she told him. They were in his bedroom and had just finished making slow passionate love. The wedding was a week away and she was due for another fitting in the morning. Irene Robinson had been so supportive and helpful and had made sure that the dresses were brought to her.

"I promise to stay out of your way when you are here," he trailed a finger down her flat stomach causing her to quiver.

"That's what you said the last time and that did not happen," she murmured huskily as his fingers continued down to her pubic area.

"I would not want to be the cause of you not making magic on paper," he bent his head and ran his tongue over a nipple, his fingers dipped inside her. "That would be tragic," he lifted his head to look at her. She was moving against his fingers and her lips were parted slightly, her black curls spread out on the pillows. "I promise to behave but not now," he removed his fingers and climbed on top of her, slipping his penis inside her wetness. "Not now," he whispered as he bent his head and took her lips with his, thrusting inside her with renewed hunger.

*****

The wedding was a crush and was highly and much publicized. The twenty-third of December dawned clear and wintry. There had been the promise of snow earlier in the week but so far there had not been even a drop.

The entire bodice was made of pearls and had a cinched in waist. The skirt itself was made out of filmy chiffon that spread out from the waist and drifted down to the floor. She wore a filmy veil caught behind her elegant chignon and flowed downwards to meet the dress, blending into the material. Her only jewelry was a pair of beautifully cut diamond earrings and gloves covered her from her fingers to her elbows.

There was a collective gasp as she made her way up to the aisle. Both her friends were wearing wine red dresses with rosebuds in their hair. Julian was wearing the traditional black tuxedo with a white rose in his lapel.

The ceremony was not long and only took about two hours. The reception was held at the manor in what they called the great hall and the festivities and dancing went on long after the bride and groom had left.

*****

"You have not told me where we are going," Kym murmured as soon as they were back inside the car and heading out. She had changed into a light blue wool dress that hugged her figure closely and matching shoes. He had changed into dark blue pants and a light blue silk shirt and he looked magnificent.

"I know," he told her mysteriously. "It's a surprise."

He took her island hopping. The experience was so incredible that she found herself almost crying that he would so something like that for her. They went to the Bahamas which was their first stop where they had dinner at the Bahamian club. Even though it was slightly crowded the Maitre D managed to find them a corner table where they had the lobster waldorf with sautéed mushrooms and drank Bahamian club mojito. They did not sleep in one of the hotels there but stayed at one of the houses there that was owned by his company. They walked barefoot on the beach and afterwards he made love to her on the soft white sand.

Their next stop was Bermuda where a tour guide took them into the depths of the caves at Blue Hole Park; they even went swimming in the natural pools in the cave.

Their last stop was Montego Bay, Jamaica. He had made the reservation at the five star hotel for one day and they were able to tour the Rose Hall Great House and spend the rest of the day in the beautiful warm water of the Dunn's River Falls.

"Any ideas for another novel?" he teased her as she rested back against the soft leather of the private company jet that was taking them back home.

"Lots," she turned her head to look at him. They had been offered champagne and caviar by a smiling and pleasant stewardess but she had foregone the caviar, never getting used to the taste. "I can't believe you did this," she murmured looking at him with a smile curving her lips.

"I wanted you to have an experience you never had before," he told her reaching for her hand with the rings on her fingers. "I know you have not said anything about it to me but I want you to know that I love you,"

"Julian-" she began but he stopped her.

"I know you care about me and when we make love it's magic." He laughed softly and brought her hand up to his lips. "I am not used to being on the receiving end of wondering if she is in love with me."

"I am not sure what I feel." She told him. "You have swept me off my feet and my head is still spinning." She reached her other hand over to close on his."You are doing something right my husband and it's making me draw closer and closer to you."

"I will continue to do so." He pulled her as close as the arms of the seat would allow them and they stayed that way until the plane descended.

*****

Kym settled strangely into her married life. She still had not given up her house but went there most days to finish writing. For the first week after they came back from their honeymoon, she totally forgot that she no longer lived at her house officially and it was when her husband came to pick her up that she remembered. She had taken off her wedding ring when she had been typing and often did that and usually forget to put them back on.

"I did not realize it was so late, why didn't you call me?" she asked as soon as he came into the office. She had spent the morning with Mrs. Willows reliving the experience of the honeymoon and had not left there until after lunch.

"I called and it went straight to voicemail and I also called the house number but it kept ringing busy," he told her mildly. He had taken off his suit jacket and hung it on the coat rack in the living room.
"Oh lord, I am sorry Julian," she got up from the desk and

came around to put her arms around his neck. "A normal wife would be at home getting you dinner and waiting for you."

"I do not want a normal wife and you don't hear me complaining." He told her taking her lips with his. He tasted like coffee and something spicy.

"If you had a problem will you tell me?" she asked as soon as he stopped kissing her.

"Definitely." He pulled her sweater up and over her head.

"What are you doing? Aren't we supposed to be leaving?" she asked as he unhooked her bra from behind.

"Not tonight." He murmured bending to take a nipple into his mouth.

She threw back her head and savored the feeling flooding her insides at the touch of his mouth. They never made it into the bedroom.

*****

They made some sort of arrangement. He moved over some of his things to her house and she did the same with hers. He was comfortable allowing her to be in her space as long as she answered her phones and let him know she was okay. The arrangement suited them perfectly and they worked with it.

She made a concerted effort to attend his business dinners with him and would smile and make conversation with the other wives there as well.

"Where do you get your inspiration from?" A well preserved and beautiful red haired woman asked her as they sat around the table having a meal.

The occasion was a cocktail dinner to host some associates from overseas. She had worn a dazzling blue cocktail dress that left her arms and shoulders bare and dipped very low between her cleavage. She was also wearing a sapphire necklace and earrings that Julian had given her a week ago. It had been three weeks since they had been married and she was adjusting somewhat.

"From all over," she told the woman with a smile, trying to remember her name.

"It's Jade," she said with a shrewd smile, looking at the beautiful black girl with open admiration. Her skin was flawless! "I already know who you are. I am married to that tall blond giant over there," she pointed to a blonde man sitting beside her husband and laughing at something he said. "Michael, he is into technology."

"You love him," Kym made the statement looking at the very attractive woman and noticing how her expression softened when she looked at him.

"Ever since I was a teenager," she said with a tinkling laugh. "We went to high school together but the selfish brute that he was he never seemed to notice me no matter how much I pushed myself in front of him."

"How did you deal with it?" Kym asked her fascinated always loving a good story.

"You are already spinning a romance novel inside your head aren't you?" Jade asked with a laugh.

"Sorry," Kym said ruefully, "Occupational hazard."

"No problem. I pursued him without him even knowing it. Men," she said shaking her head. "It was not until we finished college and he started his company that we saw each other again at a nearby restaurant and by that time had grown up somewhat from the gawky teenager he knew back then to an attractive confident woman who was not about to take no for an answer."

"He did not stand a chance did he?"

"Not a one," the woman said with a grin. "How about you? What's your story?"

"I met Julian at the opening of one of his restaurants and he did the pursuing and he never stopped until he wore me down," she admitted ruefully with a slow smile. "Very determined man that one."

"He is clearly head over heels in love with you. He looks at you every chance he gets and from what I heard about his reputation before that is quite something. He certainly has changed." Jade murmured sipping her white wine.

"He had better, I am sure he does not want to be missing the most important part of his body," she said calmly.

The woman's eyes widened as she got the girl's meaning and she started laughing!

*****

"What was all that about?" They were on the dance floor swaying to the soft after dinner music as he held her close to him. He had been staring at her all through the evening and thinking that she was by far the most beautiful woman in the entire place.

"We were just talking about our husbands." She told him, casually looking up at him and not quite believing that she was married and to him.

"What about?"

"She was saying that she could not believe how much you have changed and I told her you had better because if I found out you were cheating I would cut off the family jewels." She told him with a straight face.

He stopped suddenly and stared down at her, a little frown knitting his brow. "You said what? Oh never mind; I don't think I would like you to repeat it."

He continued dancing and after a while he asked her: "Would you really do that?"

"Without a shadow of a doubt," she told him seriously.

"There is no need to resort to violence, I am all yours as well as the 'family jewels'," he told her with an amused smile.

*****

"You look different," Gabrielle made the observation as soon as she entered the restaurant that had been chosen by her.

"How different?" Kym stared at her friend curiously. It was almost the end of January and the winter was making itself known in no uncertain way. The snow had come down heavily in the morning and had left its blanket on every available surface.

"Doesn't she look different Marla?" Gabrielle asked the other girl who was seated close to the window and was already drinking hot chocolate. For the first time, she was wearing a subdued black and white wool dress.

"If I was married to that sizzling billionaire I would look different as well," Marla said with a shake of her head. "That house alone makes me want to salivate."

"I am still the same person," Kym protested taking a seat and shrugging out of her black cashmere jacket.

"You are rubbing elbows with the rich and famous so you are allowed to look different." Gabrielle told her.

"So how is married life?" Marla asked her.

"Very good, actually." Kym told them. "He is a very understanding husband and puts up with my artistic crap and the fact that I forget where I am going in the evenings." She told her friends about the arrangement he had suggested which was working out for them. "Sometimes I feel bad about not making him dinner and even breakfast when he is going to the office but he tells me it's no big deal and they have a very good chef who would be highly offended if I took over his duty."

"Honey, run with it, which woman wants to be slaving in the kitchen day in and day out?" Marla asked with a wave of her hand.

"I think I am going to cook dinner for him this weekend." Kym said with a decisive tone.

*****

"You don't cook." Julian hung up his jacket and followed her inside the kitchen. She had called him at the office and told him to come home early. "Which home?" he had asked her.

"My house."

He smelled something baking but could not quite identify the aroma.

"Mrs. Willows gave me a crash course in baking and cooking spaghetti and meatballs and apple pie." She had on an apron over her sweat pants and T-shirt and her hair was caught up in an untidy ponytail.

He slid his arms around her waist from behind and nuzzled the back of her neck. "You do know that you don't have to do all this, don't you?"

"I know but I just figured that I can at least try and be a good wife and get my head out of my writing for a little bit." She lifted the spoon, tasted the sauce and turned and put the spoon to his mouth to taste. "What do you think?"

"I think you are a good student," he said his arms still around her waist.

"There is a bottle of white wine in the fridge can you put it on the table?"

He kissed her neck and went to do as she bid him. When she had called and told him that she wanted to cook dinner for him he had felt the warmth spreading through him. She was trying to make it work and even though she had never told him she loved him, he knew he could wait for that. He had her and that was enough for now.

She showered and got dressed for dinner, wearing a soft white dress with thin straps and spread away skirt and slim white strappy sandals. She did not allow him to do anything but told him to sit while she fixed a plate and he poured the wine.

"So how was work?" she asked as she sat at the opposite end of the table from him.

"We are really doing this?" his tone was highly amused as he leaned back against the chair and sipped his wine.

"Yes, we are," she gestured with her wine glass. "Now come on I am serious, what happened at the office today? Any major deals go through?"

"We actually won the case against the former owners of the pharmaceutical company so we are free to go along with the renovations and put things in place. Let's see," he paused as if he was thinking. "There is this abandoned building on the edge of town that we think would make a great waterfront restaurant so we are checking it out."

"Sounds productive," she said with a nod of her head, her dark brown eyes serious. "I read somewhere where it said that you have a penchant for seeing the most viable business in a pile of shambles."

"I would not quite put it that way," he said with a smile. "But I visualize what the building will look like in my head and go with that. Are we done playing the normal couple now?"

"For today, yes," she said with a solemn smile. "Now it's time for the fun part of the evening." She stood up and came towards him, pulling her dress over her head to reveal that she was completely naked underneath. He pushed back his chair and she sat on his lap putting her arms around his neck. "How do you like the evening so far?" she asked him huskily.

"I love it," he whispered, his lips claiming hers in a slow and hungry kiss.

Chapter 8

February rolled in with a massive snowstorm that made it almost impossible to navigate the roads. She stayed at his place for the duration and he had everything brought up from her house so that she could finish her writing. She was at the last two chapters and wanted to finish it before her deadline. He had turned one of the bedrooms into an office for her and promised that she would not be interrupted.

Irene Robinson was quite impressed with her writing and kept checking up on her. At one o'clock she came up and insisted she take a break. She came into the room with a maid behind her bearing a tray filled with delicacies.

"I know my son said that I was not supposed to disturb you my dear but even creative people need their sustenance." She said firmly. "Set it up over there Maggie please," she said instructing the slim black girl who always had a smile on her face.

"I had no idea it was this time," Kym stretched her fingers over her head. She had gotten up in the early hours of the morning and had taken a shower and then headed straight into the room that had been made as an office and started writing. Julian and come in and kissed her goodbye and had sent up some breakfast for her.

"Come on over here dear and we will eat together." Irene dished out the tasty smelling beef broth into two bowls and put one by her side. There were also freshly baked rolls, tiny sandwiches and a vegetable platter.

"This is delicious," Kym murmured as she tasted the soup.

"I will tell Luke that you said so, he is the chef whom you have not met since you have been here." Irene broke off a piece of the roll and spread a thin layer of butter over it. "It's lovely you are here now because I don't quite understand the arrangement you and my son have with living in two houses," she shook her immaculately styled dark brown hair.

"It's my comfort zone," Kym explained, feeling like she had to apologize to this elegant woman who was her mother in law. "I write better when I am there and there are no distractions. Julian understands." She added swiftly.

"I am sure he does my dear," Irene said in amusement her lips tilted in smile. Kym blinked as she saw the resemblance to

Julian in her smile. "James and I would never dream of interfering in your marriage and our son would not allow it."

"We don't have a normal marriage even though I am trying to be a good wife but sometimes I go on a writing binge that makes me forget where I am and the fact that I have not eaten or even taken a shower," she said with a smile. "I explained all of that to Julian and he insists it's something he can live with."

"Of course he does, he is in love with you and it's a new experience for him." Irene told her with a little smile. "I met his father while on a trip to Europe. I was a buyer for one of the biggest store lines in the country," she smiled reminiscently. "I was rushing to go to the airport and the flight was delayed and we sat there waiting to board together and he started chatting me up. I noticed that he was very handsome but at that time I had no time for a relationship, my career came first with me and I was going places. I gave him my number however and he called me as soon as I reached home that day and he did not stop calling and inviting me out until I said yes. I never regretted it since."

"Is there a lesson in there somewhere for me?" Kym tilted her head and looked at the woman shrewdly.

"Of course not my dear," Irene denied with a charming smile. "I am just telling you my love story, who knows maybe you will be able to use it in a book some time."

"I see," Kym said her eyes twinkling in amusement. "What Julian and I have is working and I am not going to mess with it."

They finished eating in companionable silence and then she resumed her writing but first she sat behind the desk and thought about what her mother in law had told her. She had never told Julian she loved him but she was getting there and she wanted to be sure of her feelings before she said the words.

*****

He made sure Valentine's Day was special. He took her to dinner at the same restaurant they had first met and they were ushered to a special booth where they were afforded some privacy. She had worn a red clingy gown with a plunging neckline which left her back and shoulders bare. She was wearing a red rose at the left side of her hair that had been combed sideways and curled against her neck. Her only jewelry was her wedding rings and rubies in her lobes.

"Happy Valentine's Day," he murmured as he leaned forward and took her hands in his. "I know I told you this morning before I left for the office but I wanted to tell you again my beautiful wife." He was wearing a dark blue suit and a red tie with a light blue shirt.

"Thank you," she smiled at him impishly. "I got something for you and trust me when I tell you that it is not easy shopping for a man who has everything," she pulled her hand away from his and reached into her little clutch and came out with a small jewelry box.

"You bought me jewelry?" he asked in amusement. She had noticed that aside from his wedding ring, he only wore a watch and she had also noticed that he collected them. She had gone on line and had found just what she was looking for: A Knights of the Round Table watch. He opened the box and his eyes met hers swiftly before taking out the time piece.

"You noticed," he murmured, taking off the one he was wearing and slipping on the one she had bought him. "I love it, thank you," he murmured looking at her strangely. He then reached inside the pocket of his jacket and came out with a small red jewelry box.

"More jewelry," she murmured reaching for the box and opening it. Her eyes widened as she took out the slender white gold necklace and from which suspended a pear shaped ruby that shone in the dim light of the restaurant. "Oh Julian!" she breathed. "I love it!"

"I am glad you do." He reached over and took it from her and fastened it around her neck, the ruby fell right inside her cleavage and he sat there staring at the red fiery stone against her beautiful coffee and cream skin. "I want to make love to you," he muttered huskily.

"They are going to be serving us now," she said faintly, feeling the familiar sensation coursing through her at his words.

"I want to take off that dress and leave the necklace on and put your nipples inside my mouth," he told her hoarsely, leaning forward and tracing the curves of her breasts revealed by the cut of the dress.

"I want you," she was trembling.

"We can skip dinner or have it packaged and take it with us and go to your house." He suggested. He could feel the sensation building up inside his testicles and his body tightening with desire.

"Let's do that," she was almost faint with desire and her nipples ached from being so stiff.

He signaled to the Maitre D and made the request. The man hurried off to fulfill his request, coming back in a few minutes with the food well packaged along with a special pastry and a bottle of vintage wine.

Julian took her by the arm and they left the restaurant. His car had been brought around and he helped her inside before going around to the driver's side. The snow was still heavy on the ground but a few days of sunlight had melted most of it.

He got to her house in record time and taking up the food stuff they made haste towards the door. All the way to the house he had had his hand up her thigh, realizing with an increased heartbeat that she was not wearing anything underneath the dress.

"I don't have time for finesse," he told her hoarsely, pulling the dress over her head as soon as they closed the door.

"I don't care," she told him pulling at his shirt. She wanted to feel his skin on hers. He took her into his arms and went with her to the bedroom, his mouth fastened on hers.

They did not eat for next two hours.

*****

Kym folded the blanket and placed it inside her basket. It was the beginning of March and the weather was a little mild. She had told Julian that she would be at the house finishing the chapter but she had changed her mind when she had seen how beautiful the day had turned out to be and decided to go up to the old abandoned house to finish.

To her surprise she discovered that it was some minutes after four and Julian had said he would call her as soon as he left the office. She had finished finally! She had gone a little over the deadline because she had changed the last chapter somewhat but she had sent the changes to Sylvia and she had been exultant with the end results and now she was finished and it was time to give her husband her total attention.

She had fallen in love with him and was planning a romantic moment where she could tell him properly. She was so deep in thought that it was when he was almost upon her that she noticed she was not alone. By the time she turned around he was already brandishing the piece of plank he had in his hand which he used to hit her over the head with.

Kym screamed out as she felt the pain race through her brain and then she remembered nothing else as she slumped to the uneven ground in a faint.

*****

Julian frowned as the phone went straight to voice mail again. He had called the house phone and it had ringed without an answer so he had tried the cell phone but she was not answering. The last time he had called her it was sometime in the afternoon and she had told him that she would see him later and then he had gone into a meeting. He called her friends and they told him they had not heard from her since yesterday.

"You know how she is when she is writing," Gabrielle told him carelessly. "I am sure it's nothing to worry about." But he was worried, why on earth was she not answering her phone?

Next he called her mother to see if by chance she had stopped by there.

"I have not heard from her since this morning Julian." Gloria Rollins told him.

He got up from the desk decisively and decided to go and look for her. No matter what they all said, he had this vague disquiet inside him telling him that something was wrong. He glanced at the watch she had given him for Valentine's Day that he had continued to wear every day and saw that it was a little past five. He would check up at the house to see if by chance she was asleep.

*****

She was not at home and the door was unlocked. He went through the rooms calling out her name but he knew that she was not there, the place was too quiet.

He had gone back outside when he saw the neighbor peering across the fence. "Hi Mrs. Willows have you seen my wife?" he forced himself to remain calm.

"I saw her heading up to the abandoned building sometime ago." The elderly woman told him.

"Thank you." He told her briefly and turned to go up there.

He remembered the time he had gone up the place to find her and admired the dense foliage and thought the place was too lonely and had thought about warning her against going there especially since it got dark so early.

"Kym," he called out as he came nearer to the place. It was too quiet, he thought, surely if she was there she would have answered. He called her and made his way up the steps and onto the front porch and that was when he saw her. His blood froze and for a second he could not move. She was lying on the floor and there was blood coming from a wound on her head.

"Please no, don't let her die," he rushed to her side and felt for a pulse, his hand tremble. He almost collapsed with relief when he felt the pulse beating weakly against her neck. He reached for his phone and dialed 911 and told them his location and the condition of his wife. He then called his parents and hers and told them what he had found. All the time he was talking he felt the helpless rage going right through him. Who had done this to her?

The place was too rocky for the ambulance to navigate so the EMTs made their way up there with a gurney.

"Is she going to be all right?" he asked as they placed her gently on the collapsible bed.

"She has a pulse," one of them said putting an oxygen mask over her nose and mouth. "Do you know what happened to her?"

"I came and saw her like this." He was hard put to answer the questions. "I'll ride with her." He said briefly as soon as they reached the ambulance.

*****

They were all waiting when the ambulance reached the hospital. He had sat there holding her limp hand and she had not regained consciousness.

They rushed her into the ER and the doctors went in immediately, leaving them outside the waiting room.

"Son, what happened?" James asked as soon as she was rushed into room.

"I don't know," he plowed his hands through his already tousled hair and felt his body vibrating. He wanted to hit something, someone for what happened. "I saw her lying on the ground when I got to the old abandoned building and there was blood," his hands were shaking and he had to clench them to get them to stop. "I told her that she should be careful and maybe she should not go up there anymore but she did not listen and now this!"

"Take it easy son; she is going to be okay." James clasped his shoulder briefly and felt the muscles bunch underneath his fingers.

He looked around the room and saw that they were all there. Her parents were sitting on chairs clasping each other's hands and looking frightened and his mother the organizer was making the rounds for coffee. Gabrielle and Marla were standing close together as if giving each other comfort and as much as they were all there, he had never felt so alone in his entire life because she was not there. His love was in the room probably fighting for her life.

The doctor came out two hours later and removed the cap from off his balding head. They knew him because they had added a neurological to the hospital and his father was on the board. "Michael, how is she?" Julian asked him abruptly.

"There is a slight swelling of the brain where the memory is housed," he said slowly, taking them all in and then looking back at Julian and James. "We have operated and stopped the bleeding but I think there is a chance that there might be some temporary memory loss."

"How is she?" Julian asked him impatiently.

"She is still out but not critical, I will know further when she is awake." Dr. Michael Jones told them with a brief nod.

"When will that be?" James asked him.

"I am afraid I am not quite sure," he said regrettably. "Julian you are the only one who will be able to stay for the night, I would advise the rest of you to go home, there is not much you can do here at this time."

*****

He kept staring at the white bandage around her head. The doctor had told him that whoever had done it had missed her temple by mere inches and that would have been fatal.

She was so still and pale with all the machines hooked up to her and he wanted to find the person who did it and break him into tiny pieces. He was so helpless and afraid. They had put in a cot for him to sleep on as the night wore on but sleep was the farthest thing from his mind; every time he closed his eyes, he saw her lying there in a crumpled heap with the blood in her hair.

*****

Kym felt as if she was drowning. Her brain was enclosed in a great fog and she kept seeing someone coming after with a piece of board. She opened her mouth to scream but the sound was trapped inside her throat and would not come out. She wanted to escape but he kept coming at her and she felt the intense pain as the board smashed against her skull rendering her helpless against the attacks and as she slipped into unconsciousness she wondered where Julian was.

*****

It was a homeless guy and the police had caught him huddled against a dumpster. He still had her blood on his hands and her laptop tucked inside his filthy backpack.

"I guess he was trying to protect his territory," the detective said with a little shrug, looking at Julian apologetically as he said it.

"She always went there so how is it that she never saw him there before?" Julian asked him coldly. They had come by a little past eight to give him the report.

"He used to be in the shelter downtown but he left there two days ago." His name was Detective Paul Moore and he was giving Julian the report, fully aware of how influential his family was in the town. He had set men on the case as soon as he had examined the crime scene and had been relieved that his wife was still alive and had not been sexually molested.

"What's going to happen to him?" Julian asked, suddenly weary and wanting to go back inside the room to be with his wife.

"He is being processed and it's up to you and your wife if you are going to press charges." The detective told him.

"I just want my wife to get well detective, I cannot think about anything else right now." He told him wearily. "I am going to need her laptop because there is important information on it."

"Yes Mr. Robinson, we will see that it is delivered by the morning."

"Thank you," he said with a brief nod and went back inside the room. She was still asleep and he saw a nurse checking her vitals.

"How is she?" he whispered.

"She is breathing normally," the woman told him with a reassuring smile.

He sat near to her and took the hand nearest to him. "Darling if you can hear me I want you to know how much I love you." He laughed a little shakily. "If you wanted me to get your attention then you certainly succeeded. You scared the living daylights out of me and I am afraid I am going to have to use the husband card and forbid you to ever go up to that building again. I know we say we are not a normal married couple but I love you and I don't want to lose you." He paused and bowed his head over her hand. "I can't lose you baby," he whispered and felt the tears coming.

Chapter 9

She was out for a week and for that entire week he did not leave her side even when her friends, his mother and her parents offered to sit with her. "I want to be here when she wakes up." He told them grimly. He looked haggard and had only shaved that morning after his father told him that she would not like seeing him like that when she wakes up.

He had conversations with her every day. The office had sent work over for him and his father had made sure he had his computer handy. Other than that he would not leave. The doctor warned him that she might still suffer from temporary amnesia even when she wakes up; that's why he made sure and talked to her every single day as if she could talk back to him.

He took breaks when the rest of the family and friends came over but never for long and he was always hovering around.

"Listen to this baby," he said softly. "We are starting the renovations to the property I told you about, the one downtown and it's going along great. I want to take you there as soon as you get out of this bed. I also want to take you to dinner and make sure you make up for not eating, whatever you want. I wish you would put me out of my misery and just open your eyes baby, I really miss hearing your laughter and the way you talk to me and you wandering around the place as you think of what to write next." He stopped as he fought the tears that were suddenly appearing. He could not let her see him cry, he had to be strong for her. "I need you so much," he ended huskily.

*****

"Give it to me straight Michael, what's my daughter in law's prognosis?" James asked as he sat with the neurosurgeon in the hospital cafeteria. He had just come from the office to see if there were any changes. It had been a week and she was still in a coma and he had seen him suffer a little bit more every day and he wanted to shout out with the helplessness of having money at his disposal and not being able to do anything. Michael was his friend as well as one of the best neurosurgeons in the country that was why he had not recommended getting a second opinion.

"The swelling has gone down and that is a very good sign and her blood pressure is normal and apart from that we just have to wait until she wakes up James." He said with a sigh. "I know Julian is suffering seeing her like this but she will get better."

"What about the amnesia you were talking about?"

"I am afraid that is quite possible." He continued, his expression bleak. "But her brain shows normal reactions to stimuli so if there is amnesia it will be temporary."
"How temporary are we talking about?" James asked him. Instead of feeling relieved he was feeling frustrated.

"It could be a day or a week or even a month."

James stared off across the cafeteria bleakly. He was fervently hoping that there was some miracle.

*****

She woke up the very next day. Julian was just about to get up and look at her when she opened her eyes and stared straight at him. His heart hammered inside his chest and he became paralyzed for a second or two before reacting. He almost sprang on the bed beside her but managed to restrain himself enough to call the doctor. "Baby, you are awake," he said his voice husky with feeling as he took her hand. To his horror she pulled away from him and stared at him confused.

"Who are you?" she asked her voice slightly hoarse from lack of use.

He was about to tell her that she was his wife when the doctor and two nurses came in. "Mrs. Robinson you are back with us," the doctor said with a cheerful smile. He had noticed the look on Julian's face and guessed his prognosis was correct. She did not remember him.

"What did you call me?" she asked.

"Your name is Kymonia Robinson and you are married to that very confused looking man right there," the doctor pointed to Julian who had retreated to the corner of the room. "You suffered from brain trauma when you were hit over the head a week ago and he has never left your side. Do you remember anything?"

She shook her head and winced. They had taken off the big white bandage and replaced it with a smaller one. She looked over at Julian and tried to remember marrying him but nothing came and she felt the frustration flooding through her.

"Don't try to force yourself to remember it will come eventually. In the meantime, I am going to examine you and make sure all your vital signs are intact."

*****

She was released from the hospital the next day but it was not a very joyful release. She did not recognize anyone, not even her mother and they all felt like crying including her. Julian took her to her house where he was sure she would recognize the surroundings.
"Bring her around sometime son but in the meantime just keep showing her familiar things." James advised him clapping him on the shoulder, his heart breaking a little at the look of hopelessness on his son's face.

She kept looking at him strangely as if he was some serial rapist who was going to attack her any minute now. He did not know what to say to her so he kept silent all the way to the house.

"Where are we going?" she asked quietly looking out the window. It was the beginning of spring and even though it was cold the flowers had started to bloom gently.

www.SaucyRomanceBooks.com/RomanceBooks

"To your place," he said forcing a smile.

"We don't live together?" she asked him curiously.

"We have a strange marriage, not a normal one as we like to think of it. You need familiar surroundings to write and I agreed to it. So we spend some time here and some time at my place." He told her with a little smile. "Somehow it seems to work."

"And you agreed to that?" she was looking him over as if trying to somehow remember him.

He nodded gravely. "Your writing is very important to you and I wanted to respect that."

"You sound like an outstanding husband." She said slowly looking out the window.

"I am a man in love," he told her with a self deprecating smile.

"Am I a woman in love?" she asked him.

"You never said the words but I think so," he said gently.

He made sure she was settled in by making her sit in the living room where she looked around the room curiously. "I obviously have good taste," she said with a little smile. She had lost weight and her cheekbones were more pronounced but apart from that she looked her usual beautiful self.

"You do," he said with a smile. He had not seen her next door neighbor when he was coming in and he knew he had to tell her that Kym was home but he wanted her to himself for tonight. "What do you want to eat?"

"Before that could I get a look at the rest of the place and the books I wrote?" she asked getting up a little unsteadily.

"Of course," he came quickly to her side.

"I can walk by myself," she told him a little coolly stepping away from him.

"Okay," he dropped his hands and schooled his features so that she would not see what her actions and words had done to him.

She walked around the place slowly, touching the furniture as if her touch would relate to something familiar. She looked in the closet and saw the male clothes there and looked back at him for a moment. Then she went into her home office and pulled her books from the shelves leafing through them with a little frown and then looking at the back page where a smiling picture of herself stared up at her."I am a bestselling author?" she asked in wonder.

"You are and your second book was also made into a television movie," he said with a smile.

"And what do you do?"

"I am vice president for Robinson Holdings; we take over defunct companies and make them viable."

"So you are rich?"

"I guess you could say that," he said with a slow smile.

"How did we meet?" she continued her questions and he was very patient with her as he went back with her to the kitchen. His mother had had the chef send over a variety of dishes and he took out a pot roast and some salad and made two plates. They had the meal there and he remembered how he had came home that evening and had found her cooking for him and what she had done when the meal was not quite finished and he felt his body tightened in need. It was so bittersweet to have her sitting across from him and not being able to pull her into his arms and kiss her until they were both mad with desire.

*****

"Could we sleep in separate bedrooms for now?" she asked him as he followed her inside the bedroom. She saw the look before he could hide it. "I know I am supposed to be married to you but I don't know you and I would feel strange having you in my bed."

"Of course," he said his voice bleak and almost breaking and without a word he left the room.

*****

Julian paced the room angrily, his pent up feelings needing some release. She did not even want to be near him, he was a stranger to her and although he knew what had caused it; that was not uppermost in his mind. He needed her and she was not available, her mind and body was off limits to him and he wanted to be happy that she was alive and at least in the next room but he could not move past the fact that she did not even want him to touch her.

*****

Kym was not sleeping. She knew she had hurt him by refusing to let him in the room with her. But how could she help it? They told her she was married to him but she did not know him; she did not even know her own name and she felt the tears of frustration coming to her eyes. They had told her that she had gone up to an old abandoned building where she had been going for a year and had been hit by a homeless guy.

Why was she so stupid as to go to an abandoned building to write? What was wrong with her perfectly safe house that she had to leave it and seek inspiration in a dilapidated building? She had almost died because of her carelessness and why had he allowed her to go? What kind of a husband gave his wife such free rein? The one who loves you totally and irrevocably, a voice whispered inside her head. Did she love him just as much? She wondered. She had not seen a ring on her finger but she guessed they had taken it off when they were operating. He had said he had been the one who found her. How had he felt? Had he thought she was dead?

She pulled the sheets up over her and closed her eyes wearily but sleep took a very long time in coming.

*****

" I left her there with her mother and stepfather and her friends," Julian had gone into the office at last not that he was going to get any work done. He was not in the frame of mind to do anything. It had been three days and she still had not gotten her memory back, three days of torture where he had not been allowed to touch her.

"You have to give it time Julian," his father told him gently, hating to see the way he looked and his slumped shoulders. The boy was suffering in the worst way.

"It's been three days Dad! Three days since I have been walking on eggshells and trying to pretend not to notice how she flinches each time I come near her. Three nights of not being able to sleep with her, hold her," his voice had dropped to a whisper and he poured himself a stiff whiskey which he downed in one long gulp, grimacing as the liquor bored a hole through his gut.

"You have to remember that she went through a traumatic experience and not to let it be about you." His father warned. "Be patient, the therapist said she is making progress."

"I want to break his bloody neck," Julian said with a growl striding towards his desk and taking a seat. He felt like crap. And he was sure he looked it as well.

"Careful son, he comes highly recommended." His father teased trying to lighten the mood.

Julian laughed shortly. "Thanks Dad," he said looking at his father fondly.

"That's what I am here for," James said before he left closing the door quietly behind him.

*****

She was sitting outside on a lawn chair when he got there. Gabrielle had called and said that they had just left and her parents had left earlier because she had wanted to rest.

"How is she?" he had asked.

"Trying to keep up with the conversation around her," she told him softly. "She is trying Julian and she did remember her mother's name today."

"Did she by any chance remember mine," he was not aware that the bitterness had crept in his tone until she answered him.

"It's not her fault Julian, you have to realize that." Gabrielle told him.

"Then who can I blame Gabrielle?" he had asked her angrily. "If she had not gone up there this would not have happened. I want my wife back dammit!" he had stopped and realized that was venting at the wrong person. "I am sorry, I am not myself."

"It's good that you get rid of it before you go home to her." The girl said sympathetically. "She needs you right now Julian even though it might not look like it."

"I know." He said with a sigh. "Thanks Gabrielle."

*****

"Hi," she greeted him warmly and for a moment she looked like the woman he had married and fell in love with.

"Hi yourself," he said with a smile, taking off his suit jacket and straddling a chair that had been left out. "How are you?"

"I think I am feeling a lot better today." She said angling her head to look at him. "Had a good day?"

"It was okay." He shrugged. "Have you eaten?"

"The next door neighbor plied me with food and my mother and the girls made sure I ate." She paused. "I need to ask you something."

"Shoot," he told her.

"Did we make love all the time?"

She had floored him! He looked at her in shock, his heart racing. "We did," he said huskily. "And we created music and fire."

"I would like to experience that tonight." She told him softly.

"Are you sure?" his voice had backed up inside his throat and he had great difficulty getting the words out.

She nodded and held her hand out to him. He took it and they stood up together. He wanted to rush with her inside the house but he knew he had to take it slow even though it was killing him to do so.

He hesitated as soon as they reached inside.

"What's wrong?"

"I want to make sure I won't be doing anything to make the situation worse." He told her.

"You won't," she told him with a smile. "I asked the doctor."

"You did huh?" he growled.

She nodded and led him into the room. The same room that she had locked him out of the past three nights. He had stayed in the other room feeling tortured and alone.

She was wearing a soft pleated blue and white dress with a blue sweater and she took off the sweater first and then pulled down the zipper of the dress and stepped out of it revealing her white lace panties. Her breasts were unfettered and he feasted his hungry gaze on them. He took off his clothes hastily and came forward to meet her. He touched her face gently and she closed her eyes and waited for his next move. He tilted her chin and ran the pad of his thumb over her full bottom lip. She opened her lips and with a groan, he bent his head and captured her lips with his, waiting for her response, his heart thundering, his body uncertain and painful with his needs. She opened up for him and his tongue ventured inside. As she responded he deepened the kiss, crushing her to him with stunning force almost breaking her in two!

She clung to him, the incredible passion racing through her body and as her nipples touched his chest she felt them hardening to painful stiffness. He swung her up inside his arms and strode with her to the bed where he laid her down gently, looking at her as if he was committing everything to memory. He climbed in beside her and captured her nipple inside his mouth, his teeth grazing it. She cried out and arched her body against his, moaning and clutching the sheets as he pulled it inside his mouth.

He went further down to her flat stomach where she had started to fill out a little bit and down to her pubic area where he touched her mound with his tongue causing her to cry out sharply.

He dipped his tongue inside her and she opened her legs wider wanting to feel more of him.

He stopped and climbed on top of her, his eyes holding hers as he guided his erection inside her, pushing inside her until he was at the pinnacle of her womanhood. She wrapped her hands around his neck and brought his head down, moving against him restlessly. He started thrusting inside her slowly at first, watching for any indication of whether or not he was hurting her. "Please" she whispered, not wanting him to stop. The feeling he evoked inside her was exquisite and she wanted it to continue.

He gathered up her hips and his thrusts became fervent and forceful as if he could not get enough of her. Kym wrapped her legs around his waist and met his thrust with hers; her body feeling as if it was consumed by a fire that was lit from within. She felt the pressure building up inside her and for a moment she found everything inside her trembled as the sensation rocked her to the very core. She tore her mouth from his and let out a scream that rang inside his ears. He came with her, his body jerking on top of hers spasmodically. They clung to each other and he felt her shaking underneath him. "Julian, my husband," she cried against him brokenly.

www.SaucyRomanceBooks.com/RomanceBooks

He went rigid with shock and he looked down at her. "Kym?" there was question in his voice.

"I remember," she whispered the tears coming down her cheeks.

"What do you remember?" he could not believe what he was hearing.

"I remember everything," she told him, her hands framing his face. "That day when it happened I was planning to tell you that I love you and I was going to make it a special occasion."

"You know me and you remember everything?" he whispered achingly.

"I remember our wedding and our honeymoon in the islands. Bahamas, Bermuda and Jamaica and Valentine's Day when we left that restaurant prematurely because we wanted to make love."

"Kym, my love," he rested his forehead against hers, his body trembling with the enormity of what had just happened. "I almost lost you."

"I know and I am sorry," she buried her fingers through his dark hair and held on. "That will not happen again."

"You got that right because I am not letting you out of my sight again." He told her hoarsely.

He held her close to him for the rest of the night and they stayed there talking for almost the entire night. When she finally fell asleep, he stayed up watching her and it was then the tears came; coursing down his strong jaw, he had his wife back and the joy was more than he could take.

Chapter 10

He took her back to the hospital first thing in the morning to be checked out but not before calling the rest of the family and friends to let them know the good news. She was back and she remembered everything.

"Girl what a relief!" Marla said with a sigh. "Gabby and I were starting to write down the crappy conversations we had when we meet in order to jog your memory."

"Now you don't have to do that," Kym told her teasingly, glad to have her friends back.

"That husband of yours suffered a lot through the whole episode and he never left your hospital bed one day even when we told him we would stay." Gabrielle told her. "You have something worth holding on to."

"I know." Kym told her softly.

Her mother cried and told her that she never wanted to be scared like that ever again.

"I am sorry Mom; I won't put you through that again."

"He is a good husband, that Julian. I never usually see love and commitment like that in a man." Gloria told her.

Irene and James met them at the hospital where the doctor gave her a thorough examination. Julian insisted on being in the room with them. He was not letting her out of his sight.

"A clean bill of health," he told them in satisfaction as they came back in the office. "What triggered the memory gain?"

Both Julian and Kym looked at each other. "We did something in the bedroom." Julian responded with a grin.

The three older people looked at them with a startled look and then his father burst out laughing. "It sure worked."

"I would say," the doctor said with a smile. "I need to make a note of that in my medical journal."

*****

"I take it you won't be coming into the office today?" his father asked with a smile.

"No, Kym and I have some sorting out to do but we will be by the house later for dinner." Julian said.

"I will instruct the chef to prepare your favorite my dear," Irene said giving her a hug.

"You gave us quite a scare," she glanced at her son. "If we had lost you we would have lost him as well."

They left them in the parking lot and Julian opened the door for her to get in. He made sure she was strapped in before turning on the ignition. "How are you really?" he asked her softly looking over at her.

"I am feeling great," she said with a smile.

"We need to talk when we get home," he told her softly as he put the car into drive.

*****

It was a beautiful sunny day and the trees and flowers were in full bloom. The squirrels were scampering in the trees and they passed a park filled with children and their nannies. It was a little past twelve when they got to her house and they went inside but not before Mrs. Willows who was looking out for them waved them to a stop and hurried over to them.

"My dear I cannot tell you how happy I am to know that you are in one piece," she said a little out of breath as she gave the girl a big hug.

"Thanks Mrs. Willows and I understand it was you who told my husband where I was." Kym said returning the woman's hug.

"I would never have forgiven myself if anything worse had happened to you," Mrs. Willows said with a shake of her white head.

"Thanks Mrs. Willows," Julian told her.

"Come on over for a bite to eat when you can," she told them with a smile before leaving to go back over.

"Nice woman." Julian murmured taking her arm and leading her up the steps to the porch. "How about sitting out here for a little bit? I am going to get us a blanket, I will be right back."

Kym sat on the porch swing and breathed in the pungent air, her body relaxed and at ease. She had meant it when she told Julian that she was feeling great. She had survived a near fatal accident and she was alive and could remember everything. She had been given a new lease on life and she had no intention of taking anything for granted again, including her husband.

He came back with the blanket and some chips for them to eat. She had told him that she did not want to go to a restaurant and he had ordered pizza which had not been delivered yet.

"I know I promised you that I was okay with you being here and with you going up to that place to write," he had joined her on the swing and wrapped the blanket around them to ward off the chill. "I went through hell and back when I found you lying there with blood gushing from your wound. I had your blood on my hands and that's not something I want to experience ever again." He had turned away from her to look out across the yard and noticed absently the gardenias rioting near the fence.

"You gave me my freedom to do whatever I please because I guess you wanted us to work," she said softly reaching for his hand underneath the blanket. "You probably wanted to prove to me that you had changed and I wanted to see that as well but from now on our relationship is going to be on equal grounds and I am going to be the wife you deserve. I love you Julian and I trust you."

He turned to face her and his hand tightened on hers. "I love you too baby and have done so for a long time." He murmured. "We have to decide however. I know you love this place and I'm willing to compromise if you want us to live here instead of at the manor."

"Why would I choose this over a sprawling house with maybe a hundred or so rooms, a huge swimming pool, tennis court and a view to die for." She teased him.

"You forget to mention the basketball court and the man made stream." He said with a smile. "What are you saying then?"

"I want to live at your place," she looked around the surroundings of where she had called home for the past two years and knew without a shadow of a doubt that she would choose being with her husband anytime over a pile of bricks and glass, no matter how beautiful it was. "I will hold on to this place for a little bit if you don't mind in case we want to get away and be by ourselves."

"What about your writing?" he asked her, not daring to believe what she was saying to him.

"I am going to be taking a break from writing and spend some time being your wife." She told him tremulously.

"You do know I do not have a problem with you being both right?" he had pulled her onto his lap and she wrapped her arms around his neck.

"I know but I want to do it and I would appreciate you not talking me out of it." She told him resting her head against his forehead.

"I would never dream of doing so." He murmured as he took her lips with his in a slow tender kiss.

*****

"You are sure about this?" Sylvia stared at her.

They were in her office where they were going through the final changes of the book before she gave the nod of approval for it to go to print. She had given the girl a tight hug and told her jokingly that she was glad she was back in the land of the living. She had also given her the piles of letters from her reading fans wishing her a speedy recovery.

"I am positive." She said firmly, settling back against the chair she was sitting in.

She had packed up the rest of her things from the house and was now firmly ensconced in the suite with Julian. He had insisted that she decorated it any way she wanted to and she had almost cried at his eagerness in pleasing her. She would have to be the one to reassure him that they were in an equal relationship.

"So what are you going to be doing with your time?" Sylvia asked her. "I know you are wealthy in your own rights and your husband is a billionaire so money is not a problem but what about your time?"

"I am only taking a year off and I was thinking about doing a historical romance. That same house where I got hit has always fascinated me and I want to base a novel there so in the meantime I will be doing research and being a wife first."

"So it took a knock to the noggin for you to realize that you need to be a good wife." Sylvia shook her head and squinted over the glasses on her nose to look at her favorite author.

The girl was so talented and her writing left you wanting more. When she had heard the news about what had happened to her and the subsequent memory loss she had been paralyzed with fear thinking that she was going to die but she had made it, thank the good Lord and now she was here saying that she was taking time off from writing. Artists, she thought with a grimace, dealing with them was like dealing with children. "I hope you know what you are doing honey."

"I do," Kym said with a smile. "I will be in touch."

"Take your fan mail with you and see how much you can respond to and I will let you know when this goes to publication." Sylvia told her with a wave. "And honey," she stopped her when she reached the doorway. "I don't blame you for wanting to concentrate on your marriage, the man is scrumptious!"

*****

"We are so happy to hear about your wife's complete recovery Julian," Peter Blagrove, a senior member of the board told him as soon as the meeting was adjourned. The others nodded gravely and expressed their relief as well. The men filed out and left the father and son still sitting in the room.

"I understand that Kym will be taking a hiatus from writing?" James asked him sipping the spring water that had been set before him by one of the secretaries.

"I tried to talk her out of it Dad but she will not budge. She is going to be doing some research for a historical novel but as for writing she is giving it a break in order to be more of a wife to me. I wish I was happy about it but what if she resents me for it in the long run?" Julian asked him.

"She was the one who made the decision son and I suppose the fact that she almost lost her life along with her memory had a profound effect on her. I think she needs to do this." James told his son. He had been very happy when they had decided to make the manor their home. He had fallen in love with the bright and beautiful girl who had married his son and he was glad they were near to them.

"She is not used to being idle Dad and I wonder what that is going to do to her." Julian said still a little bit worried. "Why don't you talk to her again about her decision and hear what she has to say?" he smiled a little bit, his expression thoughtful. "Your mother was a successful buyer for a department store and she traveled all over the world; but when we got married she quit her job and she told me she never regretted it. I even offered her a position at the company but she told me no and she found things to occupy herself. Look what she did to the hospital and the children's home downtown and now she has taken on the task of rebuilding the community center downtown. Your wife will not be idle I assure you, she will find something to occupy her time."

*****

"Darling what on earth are you doing?" Irene asked as she entered the kitchen and saw her daughter in law bent over something the chef was making.

"I think it's time I learned to cook." She told her with a grin. "And I am learning from the best." She looked up at the balding pot bellied man with the florid skin, his face shiny with a glimmer of sweat. "He is actually a fan of my books as well."

"Luke, I noticed that the produce truck has just pulled up outside could you go and see to it for me?" Irene said with a charming smile. She had come down from her study in search of her daughter in law to talk to her. She never expected to see her in the kitchen because her son had told her that his wife did not cook.

Irene picked up a snowy white apron from the hook against the wall. The kitchen was huge and ultra modern and was a chef's dream. "I never had time for cooking when I lived alone because I was always traveling and take out was my best friend." She tasted the sauce that was bubbling on the stove and smacked her lips in appreciation. "When I got married I wanted to be the best wife a man could ever have. I quit my job and started to learn how to cook and bake. James already had a chef and he did not appreciate me puttering around in his kitchen. He did not say anything because I was the boss' wife but I could see I was making him uncomfortable. One day James sat me down and told me that cooking and baking does not make me a good wife, I can be one without all of those things and besides I hated cooking." She sliced a large slice of the blueberry pie that was cooling on the side board and cutting it in two she handed a slice to Kym and they sat at the counter eating the pie. "I am telling you the same thing my dear. Julian does not care if you can boil water, he loves you for who you are and you are a talented writer who brings joy to her readers and my dear Luke is going to be offended if he does not get to cook for the family because that's his job."

"I am trying too hard aren't I?" Kym said ruefully, polishing off the delicious pie and the milk that Irene had also poured.

"Don't worry about it. I did that as well and discovered that I was not happy being someone I was not." Irene told her with a smile. "How about in between your research you could help me with seeking funding for the community center we are planning to renovate and reopen downtown?"

"That sounds like a good idea." Kym said enthusiastically. "I would love to help and maybe I could make some positive input. I also want to donate some of my royalties to the cause as well."

"Excellent my dear," Irene said with a pleased smile. "Now let's go up to my study and give Luke back his kitchen."

*****

"I tried to take over the chef's kitchen today." She admitted to Julian as sat on the large padded bench in the bathroom and rubbed some cream on her skin. They had taken a shower and he was watching her as she smoothed the cream over her skin.

"What did he say?" he asked her in amusement coming to sit next to her, taking the tube from her and squeezing some into his palm and taking her foot onto his lap and finishing the job.

"Your mother showed me the errors of my ways," she told him, closing her eyes as he massaged the cream into her skin. "She implied that I was trying too hard."

"Are you?" he looked at her quizzically reaching for her other foot.

"I would like to say no but I guess I am," she nodded. "I hate cooking Julian and the fact that I was willing to try and learn shows how much I want us to work."

"We are working without you having to do anything," he stopped to look at her. "Even if you sit around here every day doing nothing that would not matter to me. It matters to me that you are here with me and I am so thankful for that. You would never understand how much." He told her feelingly.

"I think I do," she closed her hands over his on her legs. "I guess I am trying to make up for the careless way I regarded what we had before and I am trying hard to show how much I appreciate you."

"I love you Kym and I want you to be you, not someone else." He told her softly pulling her into his arms and standing up with her. "You are my wife and you have made the happiest man in the world."

*****

"Honey, it's so good to see you!" Gloria enveloped her daughter in her arms tightly as she opened the door to let her in. "I expect to see your husband as well even though it is a work day. That man looked like he would not let you venture out by yourself again after what happened."

"I had to convince him that I was going to be fine." Kym said with a smile walking with her mother into the living room. "Where is Pops?"

"Planting some spring bulbs; with the rain we have been having he is taking advantage of it to put in some vegetables and flowers." Gloria hurried out to the back doorway and called for her husband. "Honey, Kym is here for a visit." She called out.

He joined them in time for tea and homemade biscuits. "It's good to see you up and about girl," he said gruffly giving her a big hug.

"Thanks Pops," she said kissing him gently on the cheek.

"Your mother here and I never had a good night sleep until you left the hospital. It's a crying shame that people are not safe in their own neighborhood." He said shaking his head as he reached for a biscuit.

"It was a homeless guy Pops and I think he felt threatened by my presence there." Kym said a little concern showing in her expression.

"My dear don't tell me you feel sorry for him!" her mother looked at her incredulously.

"Mom, he is not in his right mind." Kym protested. "I am just happy that I survived because it could have been so much worse."

"I still think that they should be put in a confined environment where they are monitored every minute of the day." Gloria said firmly sipping her tea delicately. "I almost lost you honey and for that I cannot dredge a single sympathy for him."

"I don't think that there is enough manpower or a resource to monitor them as much Mom but it was on me as well, I should not have gone up there and stayed there so late. I was careless and I am not going to be doing that anymore."

"Good," Daniel said reaching out to squeeze her hand. "We will sleep better knowing that you will not be wandering around that place all by yourself."

They talked about her decision to quit writing for a year. "Are you sure you will be able to do that dear?" her mother asked in concern.

"I need the break mom," Kym said with a smile. "When I am writing I am totally focused on what I am writing and I have no time for anyone or anything else. I am a married woman and my husband needs me more than my desire to write or my reading public. He has a job, a company to run but he leaves that behind and comes home every evening to me and it's all about me then and on weekends he is with me as well. When I am writing I am so engrossed I don't think about anyone or anything else. It's not fair to him and I intend to change that."

Chapter 11

The nightmares came. The day had been hectic with her sending off emails to various places to ask for funding for the renovation of the community center and Kym found that she was enjoying herself.

"I have been doing this for years my dear and it is very fulfilling." Irene told her as she got off the phone with a potential donor. "I have a committee that I work with and we meet once per week to update our progress."

Kym admired her very functional and luxurious office that had everything that an office needed. She even had a secretary who came in to work with her from nine until three each day from Monday to Friday.

"Lucy dear, send a note to Mrs. Fletcher to tell her that I can meet with her tomorrow. Thursdays are the days I make my rounds to the old ladies who are sitting on their money and have no idea what to do with it."

Kym had spent the day getting to know the ins and outs of the committee and organizing a luncheon to solicit some more assistance for funding.

She had not left her mother in law's suite until she knew it was almost time for Julian to get home. He had called her several times as usual to find out how she was doing. She had a feeling he was afraid that she was regretting her decision and wanted to make sure that she was still okay with what she had decided.

They usually ate dinner with his parents but sometimes they ate in their suite and dinner would be brought up to them by one of the maids on duty. She was not sure she could ever get used to been served by another person but she supposed she would eventually.

She had fallen asleep as soon as her head hit the pillows after they had made love. It was shortly after that the nightmares came. She dreamed that there was a large man coming after her wielding a heavy plank, his expression fierce. The more she tried to get away from him the faster he came until she fell over a piece of broken tile. As he raised his hand to bring the plank down on her head that was when she screamed.

Julian jumped up, his heart racing. He grabbed her and shook her until she woke up and saw him above her, his expression anxious. She threw herself into his arms her body trembling.

He held her to him and felt her heartbeat against his bare chest. Her nightgown was thin and he felt every contour of her body as he held her against him. He waited until she was calm enough to tell him what was going on but he had a good idea what had brought it on.

He slid back and brought her against his chest, his arms around her waist, stroking her back thankful that the trembling had abated. "Want to talk about it?" he murmured.

She nodded against his chest, feeling safe against the terror that had assailed her in her dream. "It was him," she said quietly. "I saw him coming after me and the more I tried to run the faster he came."

His arms tightened around her waist. "You know that is not going to happen to you again don't you?" his voice was tight.

"I am sorry about bringing it up again Julian," she said soberly. "But I guess it was still in my sub consciousness and it manifested itself into my dreams."

"He hurt you and I could not do a thing about it," he said trying to control the rage inside him. "If I had been there and seen him, homeless or not I would have killed him for hurting you like that!" he said harshly.

She lifted her head and saw the rage on his face and felt compassion for what he was feeling. He loved her and he was not there to stop her being hurt and he was forever going to blame himself for that. "Will you look at me?" she demanded. He did and his green eyes were turbulent. "If it was anyone's fault it was mine and I don't want you to put it on you. I am here now Julian and whatever it is, we have to learn to deal with it together. You have to try and stop treating me like a delicate glass about to break." She climbed on top of him and started nibbling at his bottom lip sending darts of desire through his body. "I am here and I love you and I am not going anywhere."*****

He called the doctor the next day when he was at the office and told him about the nightmare she had had. "It's natural that after a trauma like that for a person to have recurring nightmares Julian," he was told.

"Is it going to be a problem for her Michael?" Julian asked him abruptly. Even though she had distracted him with her body he was still on edge and he had hid his concern from her this morning while he was with her and they were having breakfast together. No matter what he had to do at the office he made sure that they had breakfast and dinner together and there was no variation, she was too important to him.

"If she wants she can see a therapist Julian," he suggested.

"You don't know my wife, she would never agree to that," Julian said grimly.

"The only thing I can tell you is that it will pass just continue to be supportive of her and make her know that she is safe. If it continues then you can suggest the therapist and hear what she says."

*****

She told her friends about the nightmare. They were having lunch in their usual restaurant. It was coming to the end of April and the weather was considerably mild and she had worn dark blue dress pants and a white silk blouse and had bundled her curls on top of her head. "I am afraid I have Julian worried." She said as she sipped her flavored water.

"That sucks," Marla said with a sigh moving her bright orange clad arm as she signaled for the waiter to bring her a glass of water. "How can you really charge a homeless guy anyway?"

"He is not only homeless but also insane and he is not going to make court," Gabrielle told them. She kept looking at her wristwatch the minute she came inside.

"Do you have somewhere else to be?" Kym asked her friend with a lifting of one brow.

"I have to be back in court as soon as the jurors are back, they have been out for more than two hours and I am starting to get worried." She said with a sigh. "Anyway back to you, after suffering something so traumatic you are bound to have some flashbacks. You think that you are going to need to see someone?"

"Like a shrink?" she looked at her friend in horror.

"Honey, I know we are supposed to be strong black women but sometimes we need a little help and kindly remember that it's not just you it is your husband as well and if the nightmares continue you are going to have to deal with that aspect of it." Gabrielle told her.

"I think you should listen to the counselor," Marla said in amusement. "She usually knows what she is saying."

Just then her phone rang and she answered it. "I will be right there." She stood up hastily and reached inside her pocket book for some money to cover her portion of the lunch she had yet to eat.

"It's okay my treat," Kym said with a wave of her hand.

"Thanks girl," she leaned over and kissed her cheek. "I am glad you are still around. I will call you girls later." She said before hurrying away.

"So how is your love life?" Kym asked turning to Marla.

"I am not seeing that guy from the party again," she said with a sigh. "He is too clingy and wants to know where I am every minute of the day. I am also relocating from where I am because they are upping the rent so now I am going to have to look at somewhere to rent."

"How about using my place to do your work? It is standing there empty and you don't have to pay me anything." Kym suggested. She had told her husband that they could go there when they wanted to be alone but the suite they had at his place gave them enough privacy as it was.

"Are you sure?" Marla stared at her in disbelief.

"I am sure," Kym told her with a smile.

"You have it all girlfriend and a lot of us search a long time for what you have right now."

*****

She started jogging again and he would not let her go by herself. Even though there was a complete gym in the manor she preferred the fresh outdoors when the weather was not cold. She woke up at six and donned her jogging clothes and he woke up with her and they headed out. The neighborhood was upscale and there was not a park in sight.

"How about a race?" she asked him one morning with an impish smile. She had bent down to tie her shoe lace and he had stood behind her admiring her curves.

"You want to race with me?" he asked her in amusement. She was wearing a purple sleeveless top and even though she was wearing a sports bra underneath he could still see her nipples sticking out.

"Are you chicken?" she asked him mildly.

"What are you going to give me when I win?" he asked her flexing his muscles and stretching his hands over his head, his green eyes quizzical.

"Very sure of yourself aren't you?" she put her hands on her hips. "The winner gets breakfast served to her for a week."

"Her!" he grinned at her. "Now who is being cocky?"

"Ready?" she asked her brows raised.

"After the count of three."

He allowed her to do the countdown and even gave her a head start. He had never told her he had been on the track team at his high school and also in college and had the trophies in his dad's office to prove it. He caught up to her easily and was ahead of her when he heard her cry out. He turned to see her on the ground and he felt his heart thudding inside his chest. He raced back to crouch down beside her.

"Kym," he called out to her urgently. To his surprise she reached up and pushed him backwards so that he fell on his back and she sprang up and raced away, her laughter loud and triumphant. He sat there stunned realizing that she had tricked him into winning. He got up and dusted himself off and saw her way in the distance.

"You cheated and that does not count," he said trying to catch his breath as he reached her grabbing her by the arm and turning her to face him.

"All is fair in love and war," she told him archly, wrapping her arms around his neck. "So what do I do? Give you the menu from overnight?" she asked him teasingly.

"You did not win," he told her sternly, feeling himself weaken as she molded her body to his.

"I did. You are such a sore loser Julian and besides you had an unfair advantage over me. Trophies for the amount of time you won at tracks both in high school and college?"

"You knew?" he stared at her.

"You have a very proud mother who happens to tell me everything." She told him using her teeth to tease his bottom lip. "So am I declared the winner?" she was nibbling at his lip and he could not think straight. He would have agreed to anything.

"Anything you want." He said hoarsely. "Let's go home."

*****

She was organizing a huge dinner party for the company and she had no idea what to do. Julian had told her that he could get people to do it but she had told him she wanted to do it. There was a catering company that they always used and Irene had given her the number. They were entertaining associates and their wives from several different states and they were going to be discussing mostly business. She had told Irene she wanted to see if she could do most of the planning herself. "If I get stuck I will let you know." She told her mother in law who gave her a nod and a pleased smile.

"Are you sure you want to do this?" Julian had asked her quizzically as he was leaving in the morning to go to the office. She had been helping him with his tie and he had stood there while she adjusted it. She had told him she wanted to do it on her own and he had warned her that it was a lot of work.

"I am sure, stop worrying." She kissed him swiftly on the mouth and made to pull away but he caught her by the waist and held her fast.

"That's my job," he had told her huskily. She had not had the nightmare since the last time and he was hoping that was it for her. "This one is kind of on the small scale because it is only about fifty people, usually there are more."

"See? I am starting off small." She told him with a smile. "I want to do this Julian."

"You know you do not have to prove anything to me, don't you?" he asked her, lifting her chin to meet his gaze.

"I know." She met his lips in a slow drugging kiss that had him being late for a meeting.

*****

She made sure she was dressed and ready and downstairs to meet their guests. She had chosen to wear a burgundy dress that hugged her curves lovingly and covered her bodice but dipped low in the back. She wore diamonds in her lobes and on her wrists. They had been a present from her husband for her birthday at the beginning of May and she looked exquisite. Her hair had been styled by a professional and was swept on top with the curls ruthlessly tamed and showed her high cheekbones to their best advantage.

She had studied each and everybody's name and was able to greet them personally.

Julian stood by her side watching her ready smile and he felt as proud as a father watching his child taking her first step.

"Mr. and Mrs. Banks very nice to meet you," she told the aging couple; with a charming smile, shaking the man's hand and giving the woman a brief hug. "Your dress is lovely and that color looks so good on you." She told the pleased woman.

They had hired people to take coats and put them away with name tags so as to avoid confusion when they were ready to leave. The caterers had done a very good job and there were a variety of entrees and main dishes because Kym had told them specifically what she had wanted.

The evening went on without the slightest hitch because Kym had left nothing to chance. It was being held in the ballroom and she had decorated it with pepper lights along the drapes and the columns and gave the place a feeling of intimacy that was greatly appreciated. James and Irene watched as she circled the room with their son and talked to the business associates as if she had known them before this evening.

"She is beautiful isn't she?" Irene murmured as she sipped champagne she had taken off the tray from a passing waiter.

"She reminds me of you when we first got married," James said with a whimsical smile looking down at his beautiful and classy wife in her dazzling green dress that suited her to perfection. He had always been in love with her and over the years there had never been anyone else for him. He looked at his son and realized that he had also found his one and only as well. "You remember our first dinner party?"

"I remember the anxiety and the uncertainties as I ran around trying to do everything by myself," she said with a tinkling laugh, slipping her hand through her husband's arm. "Our daughter in law insisted on doing the planning but at least she had the good sense to delegate." Her eyes wandered over to where Kym was talking with some of the guests and her laughter ringing out at something one of them had said. She was a natural and she fit in so well. She was not the only one watching her and she saw several of the men giving her discreet glances and her son watching her avidly, the naked love on his face apparent. "They are in love darling and I am so happy about that."

"So am I," James said with a gentle smile as his arms went around her waist.

*****

"You have made quite an impression," Julian told her as they said goodbye to the last guest. It was almost midnight but she felt charged and not in the least bit tired with the exhilaration coursing through her. James and Irene had already gone up for the night.

"I never thought that I would pull it off and I am not even tired or even feel sleepy," she said throwing her arms around his neck in her excitement. "I know what we should do?"

"What?" he asked, amused by her excitement.

"We should go for a swim." She said pulling out of his arms and opening the door. She had taken off her heels and left them by the door and raced across the grounds and headed for the pool. He got there when she had shimmied out of her dress and he remembered that she was not wearing anything underneath. She jumped into the warm water splashing him in the process.

"Come on in, what are you waiting for?" she asked waving him in.

Hesitating briefly, he started taking off his expensive dark blue suit hoping that all the staff had gone to bed by now and had not been looking at her. He placed his clothes carefully on one of the deck chairs and then with a shrug he took off his underwear and dived cleanly into the water coming up behind her and grabbing her by the waist causing her to shriek. "You are incorrigible." He told her with a laugh, his hands drifting up to hold her breasts.

She turned in his arms and hooked her hands around his neck. "Isn't that why you love me?" she asked him huskily.

"Among other things," he told her softly. "I saw you going around the room as if you had done that sort of thing all your life and I was so proud that half of what some of the business associates were telling me I did not hear a word."

"I was petrified that I was going to do something to mess up the whole evening. I almost called Mrs. Hollingsworth by her maiden name and I remember you told me that she had been estranged from her parents for years now and absolutely refused to be called by that name." She laughed as she remembered how quickly she had made the adjustment.

"You did great." He told her huskily. "Now I need to enjoy my wife for a few minutes now." He bent his head and took her lips with his. She sank into him and he could feel her nipples against the hair on his chest and he groaned with the feelings she stirred in him. The water swirled around them and he felt himself hardened against her. He lifted her up against him and slipped his erect penis inside her, enjoying the sensation of the water as he went deep inside her.

Kym wrapped her legs around his waist as he started moving inside her, his hands gripping her hips as his thrusts became more urgent. She threw back her head and he captured a nipple inside his mouth causing her to cry out as the passion tore through her body. He moved towards the edge of the pool

and held her against him as he let his control slip away from
him.

Chapter 12

The fourth of July came around with humidity and rain that threatened to put a damper on the various activities planned for that day.

Kym had been doing her research on the abandoned building above where she had her house and had become fascinated with the history so far. It had been built in the early nineteen hundreds and the first occupants; a man and his wife, had made their home there. From what she read, they had been very happy until they had lost a child in a boating accident when he was just a teenager. The marriage had deteriorated until it had disintegrated and they had gone their separate ways. What was the breaking point in a couple's marriage? She wondered as she made a notation on a pad on the desk. What happens to make a couple who had pledged their lives to be together until death decide that it is not going to work anymore? And what can a marriage survive?

Her brows furrowed in thought as she stared off into space. She loved Julian so much and she knew how much he loved her but what could make them not love each other anymore?

Julian came in just then. He had gone into his office to make a business call because he wanted to be free for the rest of the day. His parents were planning their annual Fourth of July activities during which they invited over the entire staff and friends of the family to a day of eating and pool activities and whoever wanted to play tennis or basketball. There were already tents set up all over the grounds and later in the night there would be fireworks. She had called her friends and they were coming over in the afternoon.

"What would make you leave me?" she asked him as soon as he came into the room. He had a night's growth of beard on his strong jaw and he looked as sexy as hell.

"Excuse me?" his green eyes looked at her quizzically. She was not yet dressed as it was just a little past nine. She was still in her sexy two piece lingerie that she had worn to bed last night. He could see glimpses of her pubic area because she had one foot on the chair she was sitting on.

"What could I do for you to leave me and want out of the marriage?" she elaborated turning her chair to him.

"Is that a trick question?" he came by her desk and sat on the edge of it. He had pulled on a T-shirt over his naked torso and loose sweat pants.

"I am doing research on the old abandoned house up by where my house is and I read that the first couple who lived there lost a child and eventually their marriage as well." She explained. "So I am here wondering what is a couple's breaking point."

"And you are wondering what mine would be," he mused. He came off the desk and crouched in front of her. "I would hate it if you cheated on me but then I would have to examine myself and wonder what I had done to contribute to you doing that. I would tell us to try and work it out, even if it means counseling. I love you so much Kym that I am willing to accept anything and live with anything if it means you and me together. What would be yours?"

"I have no problem with you cheating," she told him airily.

"Why is that?" he looked up at her puzzled.

"Because if you did it once you are not going to do it again because your penis actually belongs to me and I have no problem taking a knife to it." She told him with a straight face.

He crouched there staring at her, his expression one of shock.

"So aside from cheating which will never happen, I love you too much to want to live without you." She continued, reaching out to cup his hair roughened jaw.

"You are a dangerous woman," he told her dryly, pulling her down on him while he fell back on the floor with her in his arms. "I am scared to even look at another woman."

"Good," she murmured taking his lips with hers. "That's the idea."

*****

"Honey, I love it!" Sylvia said enthusiastically as soon as Kym called her and pitched the idea to her. "I even like the title: 'The breaking point in marriages'. When can I see a first draft?"

"Not so fast Syl," Kym said with a laugh. "I am still taking a break and my one year is not up yet." She paused. "But I will be doing the research and I will not tolerate you calling me and harassing me every few seconds, asking me when a chapter will be ready." She warned.

"Me harass?" Sylvia said with a mock offended tone. "I would never dream of it."
"Yeah right," Kym snorted. "What was your breaking point Syl?"

"Which marriage?" she asked wryly.

"Oh yes, you have been married three times. Is it okay for you to tell me what went wrong all three times?" Kym asked her gently.

"Of course honey, I am all better now," she responded her tone bright. "The first one was the 'trying to get away from the parents' marriage. I was eighteen and they were strict and overbearing and I guess I just did it to piss them off. He was a sweet boy who had just joined the navy and I was excited at the prospect of being a navy officer's wife. It was not yet a year into it that we discovered we were miserable with each other and we got out of it gracefully; we are still friends to this day."

"So there was no love there in the first place thus it was easy to say goodbye." Kym commented.

"I guess so," Sylvia said contemplatively. "Marriage number two was when I thought I was an adult now who could deal with the responsibilities of marriage. He was a fast talking salesman who swept me off my feet and showered me with gifts. I was dazzled by him until I discovered that he was sleeping with most of the women in the neighborhood. I threw him out on his ass and took him for everything he had, the bastard. So I guess you could say the breaking point there was his numerous infidelities.

"Now marriage number three was a work place romance and it was when I started here as an assistant editor and he was the editor. We sort of fell in love because we were spending so much time together but then I got promoted and he got demoted because his work had started slipping badly and I guess he could not deal with a woman who was going places. He took his things and left. A year after that he filed for divorce. I guess the breaking point there was his masculinity."

"So you figured that the foundation in all of your marriages weren't strong enough?" Kym asked her.

"I never quite looked at it that way but I guess you could say so and now I am married to my work."

"Is it enough?" Kym persisted.

"You sound like a damned therapist," Sylvia said with a laugh. "It is for now."

*****

"This place is unbelievable," Gabrielle said her eyes wide. Kym was taking them on a tour of the grounds. The place was already filling up with people walking around and socializing and the smell of burgers and hot dogs permeated the air. "I was here for the wedding but we did not get the grand tour. Is that a stream I see up there?" she pointed towards a little knoll and the sun glinting off a body of clear water.

"It is," Kym said with a grin. "Let me show you."

They hiked up towards the hill and stood there staring at the acres and acres of rolling parcel of land that belonged to the Robinson's. It was beautiful and well kept and very impressive.

"A person could get lost around here," Marla commented as she stared around. Both girls had come without dates saying they needed a break from men for a little bit.

"It's beautiful and quiet here and sometimes I would just come here and dip my feet into the water and let the breeze touch my skin." Kym told them.

"Okay, I have seen enough. I need to go and eat some of that delicious smelling food before I faint from hunger." Gabrielle said.

*****

"Having fun?" her husband asked as she came out of the pool dripping with water and adjusting the straps of her white bikini top. He was aware of the stir she was creating with her body and had hurried over with a towel to put around her. She waved at her mother and stepfather who were talking to Julian's parents at the far end of the main tent.

"Yes I am, where were you?" she had left Gabrielle and Marla in the water playing volleyball with some guys.

"Having a discussion with some of the guys from the office." He rubbed the towel over her arms vigorously. "Hungry?"

"Starving," she told him with a laugh as she wrapped her arms around his waist.

"Okay, let's get you something to eat and Kym, I kind of hate other men ogling you the way most of them have been doing, I want to tell them to go home."

"My husband is jealous." She teased him.

"Damn right I am," he said darkly.

"Good; now you know how I felt earlier when you were coming out of the pool with no shirt on and the water streaming off your positively hot and totally male body and every females' eyes were on you." She told him with a smug smile.

"So you were paying me back for something I did not do deliberately?" he asked her incredulously.

"Sort of," she grinned and tiptoed taking his lips with hers. "I am just staking my claim."

*****

The activities went on until way into the night and they sat there and watched the fireworks and ate marshmallows and drank wine and some people stayed in the pool until it was time for them to leave. It was almost midnight before the last person left and the cleaning crew had finished cleaning up.

"I enjoyed every aspect of the day, thanks guys," Gabrielle told her friend and her husband as they linked arms and watched their guests leave.

"You are welcome," Julian told her with a smile.
"Talk to you tomorrow, well later today," Marla said with a grin. "I need to talk about some sort of recompense for using your place."

"Don't worry about it," Kym told her.

*****

"I want us to renew our vows," Kym said to him as they were getting ready for bed later.

"What?" Julian looked at her startled.

"I would like us to renew our vows," she repeated. She had just pulled the thin nightgown over her head and climbed on the bed beside him. "When we got married it was just aesthetic and I believe mostly for the public but this time I want to do it with families and friends and I want to tell you in front of them how much you mean to me."

"I already know how much you mean to me," he told her huskily, reaching out to pull her into his arms.

"I know but I also want to say it publicly." She murmured burying her face into his chest, feeling the hair tickling her skin.

"Whatever you wish," he told her huskily.

*****

They had the ceremony the next Saturday in July. It was done at the gazebo at the house and there were only his parents, hers and her friends and two people from his office whom he considered friends.

She was dressed in a short white dress with thin straps and a flared waist and was wearing the diamond necklace he had given her so long ago.

She had written something for him: "On the day I met you I found my soul mate, the one I want to spend the rest of my life with. I have found true love; a love that has no beginning and no ending. You are my best friend, my companion and my muse, you inspire me to be better and you have added music to my writing. When I met you I thought I had it all but discovered that I have nothing if I do not have you. The day I met you was the beginning of my life and I want you and all those gathered here today to know that I love you with all of me and I will love you until the day I draw my last breath."

She looked up at him and saw the tears glistening in his amazing green eyes and felt it in her as well. "I love you," he told her achingly, clasping her hands tightly in his. "I have loved you since I first saw you and I love you even more now, my wife, my heart, my world." He gathered her into his arms and she clasped him around his neck as he took her lips with his, their bodies molded together, forgetting all the people present but giving themselves to each other.

It took a while for the minister to play his part as he declared them once again husband and wife.

They had a little brunch because they wanted to be able to spend the rest of the afternoon together. The tables were set up outside and the chef had made cold cuts and fruit kebabs and fruit juices along with bottles of champagne even though it was early afternoon.

"I am so happy for you honey," her mother came up to her when they had finished eating. "You have found a love that is so rare and I am so happy for you." She hugged her daughter to her. "He is a beautiful man."

*****

They had the entire house to themselves because both Irene and James were going away for the weekend and they had given the entire staff the weekend off. "The chef has left a mountain of food in the kitchen so you won't have to try and cook anything," Irene had told her impishly as she hugged her daughter in law before leaving. "It was a beautiful ceremony darling and it has reminded James and I that we have not been away by ourselves in a long time. Thank you."

"You are welcome." Kym told her with a fond smile.

*****

He undressed her as soon as they got inside the room. It was already six o'clock and the sun was still bright outside but inside the house the air conditioning was cold on their skin. He took his time because he wanted it to last for a long time. She pulled the buttons of the white cotton shirt he had worn and pushed it off his shoulders her hands wandering down his chest to where the hair narrowed and disappeared into his pants. She unbuckled his belt and pulled open his trousers and pulled them down. He was already hard, without saying anything she went down on her knees before him as he stepped out of his pants.

"Kym?" his voice was hoarse and uncertain as she took his erection out of his underwear and held it in her hand, her finger going over the slight wetness at the tip.

"I want to," she told him huskily, dipping her head and taking him inside her mouth. His body tightened with desire and he groaned as her teeth grazed the tip of him. She put as much of him as she could inside her mouth, pulling him in and bathing him with her saliva.

He moved within her mouth and he felt the pleasure and passion swamping his body. He endured it for as long as he could and when he felt the pressure building up inside him he pulled her up and away from him, fastening his mouth on hers in a hungry kiss that threatened to overwhelm her. He swung her up into his arms and placed her on the bed, his mouth still on hers as if he could not bear to break contact with her. She reached between them and held on to his penis, moving her hand up and down the length of him.

He dragged his mouth away from hers and looked at her with a hooded gaze, his green eyes turbulent, and his body quivering with need. He lifted her against him and took a nipple inside his mouth, his teeth grazing her and drawing a cry from her throat as her desire spiraled out of control. He released the nipple to make his way down her body until he reached her pubic area where, without stopping her, sucked her mound inside his mouth, his hands gripping her hips. She screamed and dug her fingers into his shoulders; her body bucking against his mouth, the sob caught inside her throat.

"Julian please," she gasped as his tongue entered her, thrusting inside her rapidly. He continued until she was almost mad with desire before he stopped and climbed on top of her, placing his penis inside her already wet warmth.

He lay there looking at her passion filled face, the hair that had escaped its neat chignon and was spread over the pillows and her full lips swollen from his kisses. He had never believed it possible to have so much feeling for another person but he could not get enough of her and he doubted he ever would.

He moved inside her as she moved against him and he gripped her hips to draw her closer to him as he increased the pace of his thrusts, his breathing shallow. She clasped her legs around his waist and she moved against him with a desperation that defied description. She pulled him into her, holding him against her as their passion blended together and became one.

They felt it; the orgasm beating at their bodies and pushing its way from deep down. They came together, their cries sounding inside the room as they gave full rein to their feelings and the passion coursing through their bodies like a tidal wave knocking down everything in its path.
She clung to him, not letting go and letting the feeling wash over her as she closed her eyes and savored him on top of her, his body molded to hers in sweet fusion.

It was several minutes later before they could find the strength or even the air to speak. "How are you?" he asked her softly. He was still deep inside her and he had no intention of coming out just yet.

"I will let you know when I have drifted back down from paradise," she told him weakly, her body was still shivering a little bit and she still had her arms around his neck.

"I hope you don't want me to move," he said as he rested his head on her forehead. "I don't think I can."

"I don't," she murmured, running her hands over his soft dark hair. "I want you to stay like this for awhile."

"Good," he murmured. He lifted his head and stared at her, his green eyes darkened with what he was feeling. "I spent a lot of time running around and trying to find something to satisfy the hunger inside me and had no idea what I was really looking for until I met you. You have changed me so much Kym, my wife and my love."

"I was not looking for anything like this. I had no idea anything like this existed," she commented. "Until you showed me and I never want to go back to where I was before I met you, it is too colorless and pale. With you I see a lot of bright colors and that's what I need from now on."

He met her lips with his and kissed her slowly, tenderly as she moved against him, her body fitting him perfectly and so in sync with each other.

They finally got up to eat and drink the champagne that had been left in the bucket on the kitchen counter. He made love to her in the kitchen on one of the stools, his hands holding her legs aloft as he thrust inside her over and over again, his eyes holding hers and then drifting to her full breasts. He cried out her name as he poured his seed inside her, emptying himself and holding her against him with a tenderness that had the tears springing from her eyes. She had found the reason for the passion that had been buried so deep inside her.

The end.

If you enjoyed this ebook and want me to keep writing more, please leave a review of it on the store where you bought it. By doing so you'll allow me more time to write these books for you as they'll get more exposure. So thank you. :)

Get Free Romance eBooks!

Hi there. As a special thank you for buying this book, for a limited time I want to send you some great ebooks completely **free of charge** directly to your email! You can get it by going to this page:

www.saucyromancebooks.com/physical

You can see a the cover of these books on the next page:

These ebooks are so exclusive you can't even buy them. When you download them I'll also send you updates when new books like this are available.

Again, that link is:

www.saucyromancebooks.com/physical

Now, if you enjoyed the book you just read, please leave a positive review of it where you bought it (e.g. Amazon). It'll help get it out there a lot more and mean I can continue writing these books for you. So thank you. :)

More Books By Katie Dowe

If you enjoyed that, you'll love Her Billionaire Alpha by Mia Cater (sample and description of what it's about below - search 'Her Billionaire Alpha by Mia Cater' on Amazon to get it now).

Description:

Regina has always been a strong headed, no nonsense kind of woman; traits that have helped her climb the corporate ladder. But when those same traits bring her into a confrontation with Derek, the billionaire CEO of her company, she fears she's bitten off more than she can chew. Surprisingly though, this puts her on Derek's radar in a good way, and he soon asks her out on a date. But not everything with him is what it seems. While the two get on well, Regina's about to discover Derek has a dominating alpha personality in the bedroom! Will she be able to give up enough control to keep her man? And furthermore, will she enjoy it?

Want to read more? Then search 'Her Billionaire Alpha Mia Cater' on Amazon to get it now.

Also available: Her Asian Billionaire's Perfect Match by Mary Peart (search 'Her Asian Billionaire's Perfect Match Mary Peart' on Amazon to get it now).

Description:

Leonie doesn't really believe in love.
Which is funny, considering she runs a match making service for over 50s, and her entire job is based on finding love for her

clients.

But her beliefs are about to be called into question.

One day a potential client enters Leonie's office accompanied by her son.

John Masaki is a billionaire who wants to make sure of the service's legitimacy before signing his mother up.

Upon meeting Leonie however, he soon becomes convinced he's found his own match in her.

Will the loveless Leonie be able to overcome her beliefs and pursue something she never thought she'd want?

Want to read more? Then search 'Her Asian Billionaire's Perfect Match Mary Peart' on Amazon to get it now.

You can also see other related books by myself and other top romance authors at:

www.saucyromancebooks.com/romancebooks

CPSIA information can be obtained
at www.ICGtesting.com
Printed in the USA
LVHW02s1528060518
576195LV00011B/470/P

9 781530 899562